myst

ACV 7024

D0056594

# The Truth
## about
## Bébé Donge

*Georges Simenon*

# The Truth
# about
# Bébé Donge

*Translated from the French*
*by Louise Varèse*

A Helen and Kurt Wolff Book
Harcourt Brace Jovanovich, Publishers
*New York   San Diego   London*

First published in 1953 as a SIGNET BOOK by arrangement with
Prentice-Hall, Inc. *I Take This Woman* was originally published in the
United States in the same volume with *Four Days in a Lifetime*, another
complete Simenon novel, under the omnibus title of *Satan's Children*, by
Prentice-Hall, Inc. This is a translation of *La Vérité sur Bébé Donge*.

Library of Congress Cataloging-in-Publication Data
Simenon, Georges, 1903–1989
[Vérité sur bébé Donge. English]
The truth about Bébé Donge / Georges Simenon; translated
from the French by Louise Varèse. — 2nd ed.
p.   cm.
Translation of: La vérité sur bébé Donge.
First appeared in English under the title: I take this woman, in
the vol. Satan's children, New York: Prentice-Hall, 1953.
"A Helen and Kurt Wolff book."
I. Simenon, Georges, 1903–1989 / Satan's children. II. Title.
PQ2637.I53V413 1992     91-27983
843'.912—dc20

Printed in the United States of America

Second edition
A B C D E

# — *1* —

Sometimes an almost invisible fly will ruffle the surface of a pond more than will a large stone. So it was, that Sunday afternoon at Chestnut Grove. Sundays for the Donge family had always been, in a way, historic, for example the Sunday of the thunderstorm when the beech tree crashed "just three minutes after Mother passed it," or the Sunday of the big quarrel, which estranged the two branches of the family for several months. But this particular Sunday, which might be called the Sunday of the great drama, glided by with the calm of a level brook.

François woke up at about six o'clock, as he always did in the country. He left the bedroom on tiptoe, and his wife did not hear him, or if she did, she gave no indication by so much as a quiver of an eyelash.

It was the twentieth of August. The sun was up already, the sky was the faded blue of a watercolor, and the grass was wet and fragrant. In the bathroom, François simply ran a comb through his hair and, in pajamas and slippers, went downstairs to the kitchen, where Clo, the cook, in an outfit almost as sketchy as his, was making coffee.

"I was eaten up by mosquitoes again last night," she said, showing him her pale thighs covered with red blotches.

He drank his coffee and went out into the garden. At ten o'clock he was still there. What did he do exactly? Nothing memorable. In the vegetable garden he noticed that many of the tomato plants needed tying up. He must tell Papau, the gardener, later in the morning. And also remind him not to let the sprinkler zigzag across the paths. And the beans—why were they always allowed to get so large?

The shutters of one of the windows upstairs opened, and a child's head appeared. François greeted his son with a wave of his hand, and the little boy waved back. He was wearing a white bathrobe. Marthe, the maid, was about to dress him. Below the tousled mass of hair, his face seemed thinner and more translucent, the circles darker under his eyes. He had his father's long slanting nose. It was striking. Because of that feature alone, François could never disown him. In everything else the boy resembled his mother; he had the same fragility, the same suggestion of fine porcelain. Even the blue of his eyes was a china blue!

The rooms were sunny. The house was cheerful. It was truly the ideal country place as conceived by city people. No trace was left of the peasant cottage that had been the point of departure. Now, broad

2

lawns, gentle slopes. An orchard that in spring was an enchantment. A little wood and a running brook.

Bells were ringing. The square church tower of Ornaie showed above the apple trees. On the other side of a hedge ran a steep stony road, and François could hear the footsteps of his neighbors on their way to mass. Even the hard breathing of the peasant women was audible. It was curious that you couldn't see them, but you could hear their steady cackling till they came to the steep rise; another few yards, and their words came farther apart; then they would fall silent in the middle of a word, and the conversation would be resumed only when they reached the top of the hill.

François went to get the roller in the shed. He rolled the tennis court. Then he restretched the net.

It was perhaps nine o'clock when he saw his son coming toward him with a fishing rod.

"Tie my hook for me."

Jacques was eight, with long thin legs and a rosebud mouth, like a girl's.

"Is your mother up?"

"I don't know."

The youngster ran down to the brook. He had never caught anything before, but luck was with him this particular Sunday, and a little fish caught itself on his hook. He was afraid to touch it. He was breathless, almost terrified.

"Papa, a fish! Come, quick!"

Later, François Donge, still in pajamas, his slippers soaking wet, was strolling toward the greenhouse when the cook appeared at the end of the path.

"What is it, Clo?"

"You forgot the mushrooms. . . . I can't make *poulet bonne-femme* without mushrooms."

It was the same every Sunday! François did the marketing Saturday, piling everything he had been asked to buy into his car. Everyone gave him a list, the cook's written on a scrap of brown paper.

"You're sure you put them on your list?"

"I'm sure I put them on my list."

"And they weren't in the car? . . . Oh, well!"

He went to get dressed, listened at the bedroom door. If his wife was not asleep, she made no sound.

François Donge was not tall. He was slender, but hard and solid. He had delicate features, a long slanting nose, and mocking eyes.

"Don't look at me like that! It's as if you were laughing at the world!" his wife would often say to him—his wife, Bébé Donge.

Bébé! What an idea—to call her Baby! After ten years of marriage, it still seemed odd. But the family had always called her that, and her friends, and so did everybody else.

He took the car from the garage, got out to open the white gate, and to close it again. It was only fifteen kilometers to town. There were a great many bicycles on the road. They were particularly noticeable on the Bel-Air hill, because the cyclists had to push them up the steep grade. Picnic lunches were already being spread out along the edge of the woods. François, who had a hunting license, thought that at the opening of the hunting season the broken bottles would still be there to stumble over.

The bridge. Rue du Pont-Neuf straight ahead, divided in two by the sun, and only four or five pedes-

4

trians on a kilometer of sidewalk. Shutters closed over
shop windows. Signs that appeared more noticeable
on Sunday than on other days: the great red pipe
outside the tobacco shop, the big shield of the deputy
sheriff's office. The man himself in his car, about to
start.

The grocery store, l'Epicerie du Centre, shaded by
a large awning. The smell of cheese. The grocer in a
light tan jacket. He too, in a little while, would pile
his family into the van that on weekdays was used for
making deliveries.

"Oh, and a little bag of candies for my son."

"How is Monsieur Jacques? The country air must
be doing him a lot of good. And Madame Donge? Not
too bored all alone?"

That bag of candies—François forgot to give it to
his son that day, and it was long afterward, three weeks
at least, before, putting on the same suit, he found it
in one of his pockets, the candies all stuck together.

Three weeks! People say:

"In three weeks . . ."

Or else:

"Three weeks ago . . ."

And they never imagine what three weeks, what a
few hours, may hold. Had anyone said that in three
weeks Bébé Donge would be in prison . . . a woman
so delicate, so pretty, so graceful. People didn't speak
of her as they did of other women, as, for example,
they spoke of her sister, Jeanne.

If someone said, "I met Jeanne in a shop yesterday," he said it naturally. He had simply met Jeanne
Donge, a plump little woman always in motion. The
wife of Félix Donge. The two sisters had married two

5

brothers. "I saw Jeanne yesterday. . . ." It was not an event.

On the other hand, if anyone said: "I went to Chestnut Grove and met Bébé Donge," it was felt necessary to add:

"What an exquisite woman!"

Or else:

"She is more adorable than ever. . . ."

Or:

"No one in the world knows how to dress as well as Bébé Donge."

Bébé Donge! A pastel! An ethereal, incorporeal being, straight out of a book of poems.

Bébé Donge in prison!

François got back into his car, thought of stopping at the Café du Centre for an aperitif, decided against it for fear of being late with the mushrooms.

On the hill he passed his brother's car. Félix was driving. The enormous and dignified mother-in-law of both of them, Madame d'Onneville (her late husband, before their marriage, used to write his name Donneville), was seated beside him, dressed in something diaphanous, as usual.

On the back seat sat Jeanne with her two children. Bertrand, her ten-year-old, leaned out the window and waved as his uncle went by.

The two cars drew up, one behind the other, in front of Chestnut Grove. Madame d'Onneville remarked:

"I don't see what you gained by passing us."

Then, without transition, seeing the windows open:

"Is Bébé up?"

6

They waited for Bébé Donge a good half hour. She had, as always, spent two hours over her toilet.

"Hello, Mother . . . Hello, Jeanne . . . Hello, Félix. Did you forget something again, François?"

"The mushrooms."

"I hope lunch is ready. Marthe! Did you set the table on the terrace? . . . I wonder where Jacques is. Marthe! Where is Jacques?"

"I haven't seen him, madame."

"He must be down by the brook," put in François. "This morning he caught a fish, and was frantic with excitement."

"If he gets his feet wet, he'll be sick for two weeks."

"Here comes Monsieur Jacques. . . . Lunch is served."

It was hot. The sun felt sticky; the grass was crackling with grasshoppers.

At the table, what did they talk about? For one thing, about Dr. Jalibert, who was building a new private hospital. It was, naturally, Madame d'Onneville who brought up the subject of Dr. Jalibert, not failing to steal a glance at Bébé and then at François.

It wouldn't have taken much for her to say to her daughter:

"But don't you know that your husband and the beautiful Madame Jalibert . . . The whole town is talking about it. . . . Some people say that Dr. Jalibert is perfectly aware of it but closes his eyes. . . ."

But Bébé Donge betrayed no emotion at the mention of the name Jalibert. She ate daintily, her little finger slightly raised. Her hands were works of art. Was she listening? Was she thinking? The only thing she said during the meal was:

"Eat properly, Jacques . . ."

Here were two brothers and two sisters whom fate had transformed into two married couples. In town, people always said:

"The Donge brothers . . ."

It didn't matter which of the two one had seen, which of them one had done business with. Although there was two years' difference in their ages, they looked as alike as twins. Félix, too, had the famous Donge nose. The same height, the same weight as his brother. They could wear each other's suits. They almost always dressed in gray.

They didn't have to talk to each other; they were together the whole week, worked over the same business problems in the same factories, the same offices, saw the same people, had the same worries.

Perhaps Félix was not quite so solid as François.

François was the boss; that could be felt in everything.

But it was Félix who had married the energetic Jeanne, who, at the table, between two courses would light a cigarette in spite of her mother's disapproving glance.

"A nice example for your children . . ."

"If you think Bertrand doesn't smoke in secret! I caught him the day before yesterday swiping cigarettes out of my purse."

"If I'd asked you for one, you wouldn't have given it to me."

"You hear him!"

Madame d'Onneville could only sigh. She had nothing in common with the Donge brothers. She had spent the greater part of her life in Constantinople, where her husband was director of docks. A cultured world, among diplomats and the prominent persons who were constantly passing through. Even now, Jeanne was dressed in an outfit suitable for luncheon at an embassy.

"Marthe! Serve the coffee and liqueurs in the garden."

"May we play tennis?" asked Bertrand. "Can you play, Jacques?"

"After he's digested his food . . . Take a walk first. Besides, it's too hot. . . ."

Wicker armchairs shaded by a huge orange umbrella. A red gravel drive. Jeanne chose a deck chair and, stretching out full length, lighted another cigarette and blew puffs of smoke toward the sky, which was now turning violet.

"Pour me a glass of plum brandy, Félix."

For her, Sundays at Chestnut Grove smelled of plum brandy, because she always drank two or three glasses of it after lunch.

Bébé Donge was pouring the coffee, then handing each one a cup.

"One lump of sugar, Mother? And you, François? Two? Some cognac, Félix?"

It might have been any Sunday. A torpid hour. Flies buzzing. Remarks lazily exchanged. Madame d'Onneville talking about her investments.

"Where are the children? . . . Marthe! Go and see what the children are doing."

Now and then heads appeared over the hedge—cyclists; the people on foot were hidden, although their voices could be heard.

Later the brothers would stroll over to the tennis

court and until the end of the afternoon there would be the monotonous thud of balls hitting rackets.

This Sunday was different. A little less than an hour after they had finished their coffee, François rose and walked toward the house.

"Where are you going?" Bébé asked without turning her head.

"I'll be back."

As he neared the house, he began walking faster. They heard doors slam, then sounds coming from the bathroom.

"Is it an attack of indigestion?" asked Madame d'Onneville.

"I don't know. Usually he can digest anything."

"I thought he was looking pale just now."

"Yet he didn't have anything indigestible at lunch."

The children went running past. A few moments of silence. Then suddenly, from the house, they heard François calling:

"Félix!"

The tone of his voice was so strange that Félix leaped to his feet and ran to the house. Madame d'Onneville scrutinized the open windows.

"I wonder what's the matter with him."

"What could be the matter with him?" murmured Jeanne, still stretched out in her deck chair and lost in contemplation of the smoke from her cigarette as it faded into the violet of the sky.

"I think someone's telephoning."

The sounds in the house came to them distinctly. The telephone was being used.

"Hello! . . . Operator, I know the office is closed today, but this is urgent! Give me, please, Ornaie 1

. . . Doctor Pinaud, yes . . . You think he's out fishing? . . . Ring that number all the same . . . Hello! Is this Doctor Pinaud's? This is Chestnut Grove. . . . You say he's just come in? Tell him to get here as fast as he can . . . That doesn't matter! . . . Yes, it's urgent. . . . No, no tell him to come just as he is."

The three women exchanged glances.

"Aren't you going to see what's happened?" exclaimed Madame d'Onneville, turning to Bébé in amazement.

The latter rose and walked toward the house. She was gone only a few moments, and when she returned she was as calm as always.

"They have locked themselves in the bathroom together. They won't let me in. Félix insists it isn't serious."

"But what is it?"

"I don't know."

The doctor arrived on his bicycle, dressed in brown work clothes, which he had put on to go fishing. As he pedaled up the red drive, they could see his surprise at finding the three women tranquilly installed under the garden umbrella.

"Has there been an accident?"

"I don't know, Doctor. My husband is in the bathroom. . . . I'll show you the way."

The door was opened just enough to let the doctor enter, then closed on Bébé, who remained standing motionless in the hall.

Exasperated, Madame d'Onneville paced in the hot sun.

"I don't know what's got into the two of them, not

11

telling us a thing. . . . And Bébé? What's Bébé doing? She's not coming back either!"

"Calm yourself, Mother. You'll have another of your attacks. . . . What's the use of getting excited?"

The bathroom door opened again. The doctor, in shirtsleeves, apparently in a great hurry, ordered Bébé Donge, who was standing there in the dim hall:

"Get me some boiled water . . . as much as possible."

Bébé went down to the kitchen. She was wearing a dress of pale green chiffon.

"Clo! Please take some boiled water up to the bathroom."

"I saw the doctor. Is Monsieur Donge ill?"

"I don't know, Clo. But take up some boiled water."

"How much?"

"The doctor said as much as possible."

When the cook went upstairs with two large pitchers of water, the bathroom door opened only a little way, and she was not admitted. But she caught a glimpse of a body stretched out on the tiles, or, rather, she saw two feet and two legs, and was more affected by the sight than if she had seen a corpse.

It was three o'clock. The children, who knew nothing of what was happening, ran onto the tennis court, and Jacques could be heard saying to his cousin Jeanne:

"You can't play. You're too little."

Jeanne was six. She would certainly burst into tears and go running to her mother, who, as usual, would say:

"That's your affair, dear! It has nothing to do with me."

12

Madame d'Onneville stood staring up at the bathroom windows.

"Would you mind handing me my cigarettes, Mother?"

At any other time, Madame d'Onneville would have been indignant to see her daughter lolling in the deck chair and hear her asking her own mother for the cigarettes on the table.

Now, she handed Jeanne the cigarette case without thinking. She watched Bébé as she appeared at the door and came toward them, looking the same as ever.

"Well?"

"I don't know. Now the three of them are locked in together."

"Don't you think that's strange?"

Only then did Bébé Donge betray a slight sign of irritation.

"What do you expect me to say, Mother? I don't know any more than you do."

At that, Jeanne twisted around in her chair, trying to see her sister. It was unusual for Bébé to raise her voice. But Bébé was out of her line of vision, and Jeanne gave up the attempt. In front of her, blood-red geraniums against the green of the lawn. A bee buzzing. Madame d'Onneville heaved a deep sigh of uneasiness.

Why were they closing the bathroom windows up there? And just as the windows were being closed— it was Félix who was closing them—wasn't that François's voice saying:

"No, Doctor! I absolutely forbid . . ."

The bells were ringing for vespers.

13

# − 2 −

Now he knew he was been mistaken. It had, of course, been only an intuition, but it was almost more tangible than evidence. Yet, at the time, he had paid no attention to it. He had remained seated in his wicker armchair, his eyes half closed, his body torpid with food and sun.

The clarity of his recollection was surprising, as though, foreseeing the future importance of that moment, he had photographed the scene.

It was the effect of the light. The reflection of the sun on the red gravel threw a warm glow over everything around him.

His mother-in-law was sitting on his left, half turned toward him, her scarf a violet spot in the corner of his eye. Beyond her, Jeanne, in white, was stretched out in the deck chair.

The table, with its fringed orange parasol, was in

14

front of François. Marthe, who had just set down the coffee tray, was walking back to the house. They could hear her footsteps on the driveway.

As for Bébé, she stood by the table. She was the one François was looking at with those little mocking eyes of his, which to some people seemed so hard. Was it because he wanted to see things as they really were?

His wife, for instance, with that ridiculous first name: Bébé. Her back was to him, and her body hid everything on the table in front of her. But, as far as François could judge by the position of her arm, she was pouring coffee. Graceful, undoubtedly, at that moment; a supple, nonchalant figure set off to advantage by her pale green Paris dress.

The dress was noticeably transparent. Against the light François could distinctly see her long slim legs, her thighs, the outline of her lingerie.

Bébé always insisted upon wearing extra-sheer stockings, even in the country. This woman, who for months had had no occasion to undress before a man, wore lingerie more provocative than that of a coquette.

That was his first thought, a practical thought, the way one recognizes a fact. He was neither shocked nor annoyed by it. He did not mind the expense.

His second thought, prompted by the first and by the memory of her nudity, was that Bébé might be graceful and have a pretty face, but her body was insipid, without resilience, without firmness, and the wanness of her skin was by no means inviting.

"One lump of sugar, Mother? . . ."

Wait! Even before that, she had said something

15

that should have struck him. Jeanne, who was stretched out like an odalisque, with a freshly lighted cigarette in her mouth, had said:

"Pour me a glass of plum brandy, Félix."

François could not see Félix, who must have been behind him. Félix would naturally have come over to the table. But Bébé had intervened, rather too quickly.

"Don't bother, Félix. I'll do it."

But why—when she always preferred being waited on to waiting on others? So that no one could see what was happening at the table. And, since the chairs were placed on only one side of the table, Bébé had no one in front of her.

It was a little later that she had asked:

"One lump of sugar, Mother?"

François had not given a start. He had not frowned. His movement was almost imperceptible. A sidewise glance at Madame d'Onneville. Who half opened her mouth, like someone on the point of making a remark but changes her mind, deciding it isn't worth the trouble. If she had spoken, she would undoubtedly have said:

"Don't you know by this time, after twenty-seven years, how many lumps of sugar I take in my coffee?"

She didn't say it. But it would have been like her.

In all probability, Bébé first filled the five coffee cups. At Chestnut Grove they always used lump sugar, individually wrapped in paper. That was why she felt the need of saying something: to fill a silence, to distract attention, as a magician does from a trick. Were her hands trembling a little? Was her throat tight?

François, who had seen her only from behind,

16

could not tell. At any rate, in the hollow of that hand which everyone admired, there must have been a little piece of paper containing white powder.

"One lump of sugar, Mother? . . . And you, François? Two?"

She knew how many lumps her husband took. But, with her back to them, she had to make sure where each one was, to hear them speak while she removed the paper from the two lumps of sugar and poured the white powder from the other paper.

The proof was that then she failed to ask her sister or Félix the same question. Another clue (in thinking back, one might find a hundred) was that she forgot to pour the plum brandy for Jeanne after stopping Félix from doing it.

François, while all this was happening, had not thought about them particularly, or realized their significance, yet he had been vaguely conscious of something ambiguous, abnormal, even menacing.

Why hadn't he done something? Probably because it is always like that with warnings of this kind.

Even after he drank his coffee and noticed a peculiar taste . . . He had almost mentioned it. Why had he not? Because it was his way, to keep things to himself. Because there was nobody there with whom he had anything in common, with the exception of his brother Félix.

He didn't fool himself. He was a practical man, devoid of imagination. He was no more at home at Chestnut Grove than in a hotel room. And there was nothing of him in his son's face, except for the nose. Moreover, for some time now, even his son had seemed to shrink from him.

When he drank his coffee without saying anything, Bébé, finally sitting down, must have felt relieved.

There was not the slightest intimation of poisoning. It was the usual family Sunday afternoon, with all its sumptuous emptiness and long stretches of silence, which each one, sunk in his garden chair, traveled in his own way. The one who first opened his mouth seemed to be the first to arrive from an uneventful journey.

François was dozing when he began to feel discomfort. He followed its course through his body with amazement.

Indigestion, he thought. It's the coffee. I wonder if I'll have to go in and vomit.

The prospect annoyed him, and then a chill gripped the nape of his neck. And his temples began throbbing.

He had never been ill. Had he perhaps stayed in the sun too long that morning rolling the tennis court?

It was getting worse. He was clammy. He seemed to feel the cord in his spinal column.

He disliked being disturbed, and tried to avoid disturbing others. So he rose without saying anything, afraid only that he would not be able to reach the house in time. While he crossed the sunny drive, where the red gravel seemed more aggressive than ever, he said to himself:

"It can't be possible. . . ."

The symptoms of arsenic poisoning. He recognized them. He was a chemist. In that case . . .

In the dining room he almost ran into Marthe, who was putting away the lunch dishes. He didn't speak to her, but was aware of her dismay as he walked past. He would have to hurry. In the bathroom, he had just time to put his finger down his throat.

He vomited a little and felt a burning sensation. He kept on vomiting, on the tile floor, but that didn't matter. Now frightened, feeling himself stiffening with cold, he shouted out the window:

"Félix!"

He was afraid of dying. In severe pain, he knew the terrible efforts he would still be called upon to make, and yet he could not help thinking:

So, she really did it. . . .

Bébé had never threatened to kill him. He had never said to himself that someday she would poison him. Yet he was not surprised. Nor was he indignant. No, he felt no animosity toward his wife.

"What's the matter, François?"

"Phone the doctor . . . Hurry . . ."

Poor Félix! He would much rather have endured the pain himself than see his brother suffer.

"Is he coming? . . . Good. Go get me some milk from the refrigerator . . . Say nothing to the servants . . ."

He had time to be pleased with himself: Wasn't he thinking of everything? Wasn't he doing the right things, not losing his head? And the three women were still there, outside, around the orange parasol!

What did Bébé feel as she looked at the open window?

That was it, then. For years . . . And no one had suspected, not even he! . . . He had been deceived like other men; he had seen nothing.

19

That wasn't true. As with the lumps of sugar, hadn't he felt at times something like a warning? . . . Yet he had preferred not to understand. . . .

He did not lose consciousness, but everything became confused—the doctor, terrified Félix, the vomiting, the cold tile floor, his arms being rhythmically moved up and down by someone sitting on his chest.

The doctor was saying to Félix:

"Your brother was poisoned by a very strong dose of arsenic. He's lucky that . . ."

"It's impossible! Who would have done it?" cried Félix. "We've spent the whole day by ourselves. No one's been here."

François, not fully realizing his condition, smiled ironically.

"We must phone for an ambulance. What private hospital do you prefer?"

He was racked by excruciating cramps. Fire ran through his innards. Yet, making a wry face, he summoned the strength to say:

"Not a private hospital."

Because of Dr. Jalibert. His hospital wasn't finished. If François went to any other, Jalibert would be offended, because François would be putting himself into the hands of one of Jalibert's colleagues. People in town wouldn't understand.

"The city hospital . . . St. John's . . ."

Again the voice of the doctor, who was a good, conscientious man:

"I'll have to inform the authorities. It's Sunday, so the courthouse will be closed. But I know the deputy public prosecutor. . . . The number's 18-80, I think. Will you please get it for me, Monsieur Donge."

It was then that François said, or thought he said: "No, Doctor! I absolutely forbid . . ."

A family had just passed on the other side of the gate. The father was carrying a small child on his shoulders. The mother was dragging another behind her. And there seemed to go along with them the smell of dust and sweat and leftover wilted ham sandwiches and watered wine in gourds.

The bells were ringing again, perhaps for the end of vespers, when the ambulance appeared, white with a red cross and little opaque windows along the sides, at the open gate. Paying no attention to the three women, it went on to the front door, and a man in a white coat jumped out.

One's throat tightened. This was tragedy suddenly entering the house in the form of a white ambulance, an insigne, and a uniform.

Madame d'Onneville's ample bosom rose. Sternly, the mother regarded her daughter, who remained impassive.

"You don't seem to be much troubled by what is happening. . . ."

Bébé's calm horrified her. She looked at her with wide eyes, as if she'd never seen her before.

"It's been a long time since François and I had anything in common."

It was Jeanne's turn to scrutinize her sister. She did so with a more penetrating eye. It made Bébé uncomfortable. Jeanne suddenly got out of her chair and ran toward the house, saying:

"I'm going to find out!"

21

The ambulance driver and the doctor were hold-ing François between them. He was deathly white, and his head drooped on his shoulder.

"Félix!" cried Jeanne, seizing her husband's arm.

"Leave me alone."

"What's happened?"

"You want to know what's happened? You want to know?"

Félix was yelling in his effort not to burst into sobs, not to strike his wife, and to help the two men lift François into the ambulance.

"Your bitch of a sister poisoned him!"

Never before had he uttered such a coarse word. He abhorred profanity.

"Félix, what are you saying? . . . Listen . . ."

Bébé Donge was no more than five steps away, standing very straight, the sunlight in her hair, which was made even fairer by artificial means. She was ethe-real in her green dress, one hand hanging at her side, the other pressed against her little none-too-firm breasts. She was watching.

"Bébé! Did you hear what Félix . . ."

"Jeanne . . . Bébé . . ."

It was Madame d'Onneville, who had also heard. Her whole diaphanous mass began to sway. In another moment she would collapse, but she held out as long as possible because she felt sure no one would pay the slightest attention to her.

"Félix! Let me go with you."

He looked at Jeanne with an expression that was hard and full of hate, as if she were Bébé, or as if she, like her sister, was a poisoner.

The ambulance was starting. The doctor, in the

front seat, signed to the driver to stop for a moment and leaned toward Jeanne.

"You had better keep an eye on your sister until . . ."

The rest was lost. The driver, thinking he had finished, had started again and was making a sharp turn.

The children came running up from the tennis court. Jacques stopped short a few steps from his mother. Had he heard something? Was it the sight of the ambulance that suddenly froze him like that?

"Mama, what's happened to Uncle François?"

It was Bertrand, pulling at his mother's dress, and Jeanne let herself sink down on the grass.

"Marthe!!" called Bébé. "Marthe!! Where in the world are you?"

"Here I am, madame."

She was wiping her eyes on the corner of her apron. She probably knew nothing at all, but she could weep with perfect justification because an ambulance was leaving the house.

"Will you please look after Jacques. Take him for a walk to Four Pines."

"I don't want to," the boy protested.

"Did you hear me, Marthe?"

"Yes, madame."

And Bébé, still so exactly her usual self that it was like a nightmare, began walking toward the front door.

"Eugénie . . ."

It was the first time in many years that Jeanne had called her sister by her baptismal name. Bébé, like her mother, was Eugénie.

"What do you want?"

"I must speak to you."

"I have nothing to say to you."

She went slowly up the steps. Was she really more affected than she wished to appear; were her legs trembling under the green dress? Jeanne followed her. They met again in the dining room, where the shutters were kept closed during the heat of the day.

"You might at least answer me."

Bébé turned toward her listlessly. Her eyes already showed the tragic serenity of those who know that no one will ever understand them again.

"What do you want to know?"

"Is it true?"

"That I poisoned him?"

She pronounced the word simply, without disgust, without horror.

"It was he who said that, wasn't it?"

There was an intention there that Jeanne sensed but could not quite fathom. The *he* had a capital H. Bébé was not speaking of a man like ordinary men, nor even of her husband. She was speaking of Him.

And she did not resent His having accused her. Jeanne was perhaps wrong; she didn't think she was much of a psychologist. Yet that apparent contentment . . . Yes, Bébé seemed to be content that François had accused her of trying to poison him. She stood waiting for her sister's answer, one foot poised on the first step of the stairs. Her lizardskin shoes were green like her dress, but a deeper shade.

"It's true, isn't it?"

"Why wouldn't it be true?"

Considering the conversation ended, she began

24

climbing the stairs, without haste, while with a peculiarly feminine gesture she held up her long, full skirt.

"Bébé!"

She continued up the stairs.

"Bébé, I hope you're not going to . . ."

She had almost reached the top and was now in shadow. She waited a moment, then turned.

"You needn't worry, dear. . . . If anyone asks for me, I'll be in my room."

That room, which was hung with satin, looked like the inside of a candy box. Bébé looked at herself in the three-panel mirror, looked at herself from head to foot, and with a familiar movement slightly lifted her hair, disclosing her shaved armpits. An opening, left intentionally, between the closed shutters let in a single ray of sunlight, which drew a triangle on a small lacquered secretary. A little bedside clock showed ten minutes to four.

Bébé Donge sat down at the secretary, with an air of weariness opened it, and drew toward her a tablet of pale blue paper.

She looked as if she had a difficult letter to write. With the point of her pen on her chin, she sat staring at the shutters, behind which flies were buzzing in the sunlight.

Finally she began to write, in a schoolgirl hand:

"1. Be sure not to forget his medicine every morning. Increase the number of drops progressively after the first cold days.

"2. Every third day give him hot chocolate instead of oatmeal for his breakfast, but do not sweeten it as much as the last time (three lumps are enough).

"3. Don't let him wear his suede shoes again; they

are too porous. See that he doesn't walk in the wet grass mornings and evenings. Watch this especially in September. He should not go out in foggy weather.

"4. Don't let newspapers accumulate in the house, especially a newspaper that has been used to wrap food. Don't talk with others in corners or behind doors. Try not to look so worried.

"5. In his wardrobe, to the left, there is . . ."

Sometimes she raised her head and listened. Once, she heard someone on the stairs, and from the hall came her sister's voice, saying timidly:

"Are you there?"

"Don't bother me. I'm busy."

Jeanne must have heard the scratching of Bébé's pen on the stationery, because after a moment she went downstairs again.

"12. Clo is a gossip, so be sure that she never goes to the village to do the marketing. Order everything by phone. Let the delivery men in yourself and *never* when Jacques is around."

A car . . . No, it wasn't the right one yet. It went on up the road without stopping at Chestnut Grove. The wind must have shifted as the sun went down, because now she could hear the sounds of a radio, drifting up from the little restaurant-bar down in Ornaie. . . .

The ray of sunlight on the secretary had grown duller, as though mixed with oil.

"No, of course she isn't crazy, Mother. . . . There are certainly things we don't know. . . . Bébé's always been secretive."

"She was always so delicate."

26

"That's no excuse. If you hadn't spoiled her . . ."

"Be quiet, Jeanne. This is no time to . . . You really think she . . . Why, then . . ."

Madame d'Onneville had recovered enough to sit up and watch the gate, which had been left open.

"They'll come . . . It isn't possible. Think of the disgrace!"

"Calm yourself, Mother . . . What do you expect me to do?"

"No one can make me believe that at lunch, right in front of me, my own daughter . . ."

"But she did, Mother."

"So you're turning against her too?"

"I'm not, Mother. . . ."

"It's true, you're married to a Donge! . . . As for me, I'll never be able to face anyone again. Tomorrow it will be in all the papers. . . ."

"Day after tomorrow, because today's Sunday and . . ."


The appearance of a city taxi was almost as alarming as that of the ambulance had been. It went past the open gate. Dr. Pinaud, who was in it, leaned forward to direct the driver. The latter, deciding that it was impossible to turn into the hospital grounds, simply backed up a little way and stopped.

The hospital was a fine old sixteenth-century building with high pointed roofs, the tiles turned multicolored by time. White walls, enormous windows with tiny panes, and an interior court shaded by plane trees. Old men in blue jackets and pants were wan-

27

dering from bench to bench, some with bandaged legs and leaning on canes; others, with bandaged heads, supported by nursing sisters in big white coifs.

François had been taken into the operating room. Dr. Levert, notified, was there ahead of him and had already put on rubber gloves. Everything was ready for stomach pumping and the rest of the treatment.

François had sworn to himself that he would not cry out. Two injections of morphine had not taken away all his power of thought, and he could still feel ashamed to lie there naked as a corpse in front of a pretty nurse. He wanted to reassure Félix, who was almost out of his mind. The doctor was threatening to eject Félix from the room.

His eyes were closed, when all at once he saw the scrap of paper. He was no longer in St. John's Hospital, near the canal, but at Chestnut Grove, and the red of the gravel formed an immense sunny pool. Across it the legs of the garden table cast their shadows. And there, between two of the shadows, lay a crumpled scrap of paper. *He had seen it.* The proof was that he was seeing it again, and he was not delirious. Where could Bébé have hid it after letting the poison slide into the cup? She had no pocket in her dress. She had no handbag with her. She had rolled it into a ball in her moist palm and, thinking that a scrap of paper would not be noticed in a garden, had let it fall to the ground.

Was the paper still there? Had she come back for it in order to burn it?

"Try to lie perfectly still for a moment . . ."

He gritted his teeth, but to his great chagrin a cry escaped him. Félix heaved a sigh.


"Is Madame Donge at home?"

He was tall, thin, and dressed in a gray woolen suit of poor quality and badly cut. The suit quite plainly came from a cheap ready-to-wear store. He held his hat in his hand; the doctor kept his on his head.

"You want to see my sister, don't you? She is in her room. I'll call her, if you like."

"Tell her, Sergeant Janvier of the Homicide Squad."

It was Sunday. The chief inspector was attending a billiard match in the next town. The deputy public prosecutor was detained at home by his wife's imminent confinement, though he kept in telephone contact.

"You locked the door?"

"Of course not. Just turn the knob."

Naturally! Jeanne in her excitement was turning the doorknob in the wrong direction. Bébé still sat at her secretary, reading over what she had written.

"How many are there?"

"Only one."

"Does he want to take me away at once?"

"I don't know."

"Tell Marthe I want to see her."


"My sister will be down in a moment."

The doctor was speaking in a low voice to the ser-

29

geant, who seemed overawed by the perfectly waxed dining-room floor. Jeanne noticed that there was an "invisible" patch on the vamp of one of his shoes.

"Get out my pigskin suitcase, Marthe . . . No. I'd better take the airplane one, it's lighter. . . . Pack enough lingerie for a month, two dressing gowns, my . . . What are you crying for?"

"Nothing, madame."

"Dresses? Let's see . . ."

She opened a wardrobe to choose the dresses she would need.

"I've left you instructions about everything. Write me every other day and let me know how things are. Don't be afraid to put down even the most trifling details. . . . Where did you leave Jacques?"

"He is with his cousins."

"What have you told him?"

"That Monsieur Donge had an accident, but that it isn't serious."

"What are they doing now?"

"Jacques is showing them how he caught a fish this morning."

"I am going downstairs. As soon as the suitcase is ready, bring it down to me."

The sight of her bed made her long to lie down, if only for a moment.

"Marthe . . . By the way, I almost forgot. If Monsieur Donge comes back before I do . . ."

The maid burst into sobs.

"Oh, heavens! Can't I say two consecutive words to you? . . . I want you to see to it that, for Jacques, nothing is changed. Follow my directions. You understand? . . . There are little things Monsieur Donge does not consider important."


"Excuse me for keeping you waiting, Inspector."

"Sergeant . . . I came on ahead. The inspector and the others will be here shortly."

He took a large silver watch out of his pocket.

"While waiting, if you will allow me, I could ask you some preliminary questions, so as to . . ."

"Shall I wait outside?" asked the doctor, still in his fishing clothes. The polished floor showed the scuffs of his hobnailed boots.

"Yes, if you please. They'll take your statement when they come."

From his pocket, the long lean sergeant drew a ridiculously little notebook and then seemed at a loss to know what to do with it.

"It will be easier for you to write in my husband's study. Would you come this way."

Might not the whole mechanism suddenly stop, and wouldn't she then fall flat on the floor? In that case, there would have been no more Bébé Donge.

31

## – 3 –

After all the wretched fears, the echoing voices, the medical attention, the sweating, after the sickening disorder and the foul odors of the first hours, it was good, in a hospital, calm at last, to be stretched out in cleanliness, surrounded by nothing but cleanliness— white sheets, spotless floor, medicine bottles neatly arranged on a glass tray.

Instead of the noisy bustle of nurses, the cries of patients whose wounds were being dressed, now, in the corridors, there was no sound but the soft footsteps of the nuns and the jingling of their rosaries.

François felt emptier than he'd ever felt before, empty and clean, like an animal a butcher has just relieved of its entrails and whose hide he has carefully washed and scraped.

"May I come in? . . . I have just seen Doctor Levert, who tells me you are out of danger."

All smiles, Sister Adonie came into the room, to see how the patient was doing. She was tiny and plump and had a decided accent, the accent of Cantal, as far as François could judge. He looked at her as he looked at everything, without putting himself out for her, without thinking himself obliged to smile, and Sister Adonie, like so many others, must have got the wrong impression.

Did she think it was because he was in despair over his wife's act, or did she simply conclude that he didn't like nuns? She set about taming him at once.

"Would you like me to open your window? From your bed you'll be able to see a little bit of garden. You've been given the best room, number six. . . . For us, that makes you Monsieur Six. . . . You see, we never use our patients' names. Why, Number Three, who left yesterday, was here for several months, and I never knew his name."

Kindly Sister Adonie! She did everything she could, never dreaming that François looked at her as he did because, in spite of himself, he saw her without her gray frieze robe of the order of St. Joseph.

It was quite involuntary. The moment she entered, he had wondered how she would look without the uniform which idealized her, without her cornet. She'd be a stocky peasant woman, her thin hair pulled back into a knot, her stomach sticking out under her blue cotton apron. A short skirt—too short—and black woolen stockings . . .

He imagined her with her hands on her hips,

33

standing in the doorway of a peasant cottage among chickens and geese.

And Sister Adonie, seeing him so indifferent to her actual presence, was more and more misled.

"Poor man . . . You mustn't judge her too hastily. You mustn't be too bitter against her. If you only knew the things that go on in women's heads sometimes! . . . Why, we had one here in the next room. She'd tried to kill herself by jumping out the window. She kept insisting that she was a criminal, that she had smothered her baby one night because he was crying. Well, believe it or not her baby had been born dead. She'd never even seen it. And it was several months later, though during all that time she'd seemed perfectly normal, that one fine morning she woke up imagining she'd committed the crime."

"Is she cured?" he calmly inquired.

"She has another child. . . . She comes to see us sometimes when she is taking a walk with him in this neighborhood. . . . Sh! I think I hear someone in the corridor. It must be for you."

"It's my brother," François said without hesitation.

"Poor soul! He spent the whole night in the hospital corridors. It's against the rules, but the doctor was sorry for him. . . . He didn't leave until six o'clock, after they'd assured him you were out of danger. . . . Let me have your wrist . . ."

She took his pulse, seemed satisfied.

"I'll let him come in, but he mustn't stay more than a few minutes, and I want you to promise me to be good."

"I promise," he said, smiling at last.

Félix hadn't slept a wink. At six o'clock, as Sister

34

Adonie said, they had put him out of the hospital, and he'd gone home to take a bath, shave, and change his clothes. Already he was back, standing there at the end of the corridor, seething with impatience because he had to wait, like any stranger, for permission to see his brother.

"You can go in. But not more than five minutes, remember! And say nothing that might excite him."

"Is he calm?"

"I don't know. He's not like other patients."

The two brothers did not shake hands. They didn't have to.

"How do you feel?"

A simple movement of the eyelids to say that everything was all right. And finally the question Félix was expecting:

"Have they arrested her?"

"Yesterday evening . . . Fachot himself came out to Chestnut Grove. . . . I was afraid it would be embarrassing. But not at all. She behaved very well."

Fachot, the deputy public prosecutor, was a friend. Almost every week they ran into him at some bridge party.

"He was the one who was embarrassed. He kept stuttering. . . . You remember how he is . . . never knows what to do with his arms, where to put his hands. . . ."

"And Jacques?"

"They kept him out of the way. . . . Jeanne is at the house with the children."

Félix was not being frank. François felt it. But he was charitable and pretended not to notice. What were they hiding from him?

35

Almost nothing. Only one small detail. It was true that everything had gone off well. The irruption of the law at Chestnut Grove had, in fact, been nothing more than a formality. Fachot had come in his own car with his recording clerk; and the newly appointed medical expert, not having a car of his own, had followed in a taxi. The others waited for him at the gate, to consult together before continuing to the house.

Bébé, who had put on her hat, coat, and gloves, and whose suitcase was already on the front steps, immediately came out to meet them.

"How do you do, Monsieur Fachot. [Ordinarily she called him Fachot, since they were quite good friends.] I'm sorry to bother you. . . . My mother and sister are with the children. I think it would be best for us to leave at once. I deny nothing. I poisoned François with arsenic. Look! You can see the paper it was wrapped in from here."

Calmly, she walked over to the table with the umbrella and from the red gravel, darker now in the waning light, picked up a tiny piece of tissue paper rolled into a ball.

"I suppose you could put off questioning my mother and sister, and the servants, until tomorrow?"

General conference. The sergeant, wanting to make himself agreeable, said: "I have already questioned Madame Donge. I'll have my report ready by this evening."

"You have a taxi waiting?" Fachot asked him. "Then you can take charge of Madame Donge?"

No one in Ornaie suspected tragedy, in spite of all the parked cars outside the gate. People merely thought it was a cocktail party at Chestnut Grove.

Their business finished, all they had to do was to go down and get into the cars.

"Will you bring my suitcase, Marthe."

She was walking toward the gate, ahead of the others, when Jacques came running up to her, a lock of hair falling over his forehead. No one was supposed to have told him anything. Yet, looking at his mother with respectful surprise, he asked:

"Is it true you're going to jail?"

He was more curious than frightened. She smiled as she bent down to kiss him.

"Can I come see you?"

"Of course, Jacques . . . if you're a good boy."

"Jacques! Jacques!" Jeanne was calling in alarm.

"Now run back to Aunt Jeanne. And promise me you won't go fishing again."

That was all. She climbed into the taxi, and the gentlemen of the law, before getting into their own cars, bowed to her.

Félix arrived a little later in his own car. He was in a state of feverish haste. François's condition was still critical. He found his wife and mother-in-law in the house, their eyes red, and asked harshly:

"Where is she?"

The children were eating, and Jeanne rose and said with quiet authority:

"Come out into the garden."

She knew that expression, that spasmodic trembling of his lips.

"Listen, Félix, it's better for us not to talk about it now. . . . I don't know what went on in my sister's head. I wonder if she didn't suddenly go crazy. . . . Bébé has never been like other people. . . . You know

37

how fond I am of François. Go back to him. Stay at our place for a few days. . . . I think it's better for me to remain here with the children."

She looked at him more gently.

"It will be better like that, don't you think?"

She wanted to kiss him, but this wasn't the time or place.

"Better go now! Tell François that Marthe and I will look after Jacques. Good night, Félix."

An hour or so later, Madame d'Onneville telephoned for a taxi. She insisted that Chestnut Grove was stifling her. She could think of nothing but the poisoning, and she wouldn't be able to sleep all night.

"Besides, I haven't any of my toilet things with me."

She left and went home to her apartment, which consisted of an entire floor of eight rooms in one of the finest apartment houses in the city.

"Nicole . . . we're leaving for Nice tomorrow."

"Very well, madame."

Nicole was a pest, and, although the maid was only nineteen, the two women quarreled like girls of the same age.

"Does madame remember that her white wool coat is at the cleaner's?"

"You'll have to go first thing in the morning and get it."

"And if it isn't ready?"

"Then take it as it is. Now help me start packing."

And so, for Madame d'Onneville the Lord's Day ended in a tumultuous sorting out of dresses and lingerie.

"Isn't madame afraid it will be too hot in Nice at this time of year?"

"It's because of that butcher's boy you say that, isn't it? Well, butcher boy or no butcher boy, you're coming with me to Nice, my girl."

Next day she sent a telegram to Madame Berthollat, who ran a pension on the Promenade des Anglais where Madame d'Onneville spent several weeks each year.

Félix, whose nerves were all the more on edge for not having slept, paced up and down the room as he said:

"I wonder why she did it. . . . I'm trying my best to understand . . .Unless . . ."

And François, as calm as ever, looked at him very much as he had looked at Sister Adonie a short time before.

"Unless what?"

"You know what I mean . . . if she found out about Olga Jalibert."

Félix flushed. The two brothers did everything together. They worked together. Together they had built up the various enterprises that were known in the city as the Donge interests. Together they got married, and married sisters. And together, out of their common funds, they had renovated Chestnut Grove, which the two families occupied in turn during the summer months. Yet it took a catastrophe to bring Félix to the point of mentioning, now, the name Olga Jalibert, who, as almost everyone in town knew, was François's mistress.

François, with no sign of emotion, remarked:

"Bébé isn't jealous of Olga."

Félix gave a start. He turned to his brother with rather more eagerness than he intended. He had been struck by François's voice, by its calm, its assurance.

"She knew?"

"Long ago."

"You told her?"

François's face was suddenly contorted by pain. Once more a fiery arrow was piercing him, which meant another hemorrhage.

"It's too complicated," he managed to stammer. "I'm sorry. Will you call the nurse?"

"May I stay?"

François had just enough strength left to shake his head.

Again he surrendered himself to pain and medical attention. His respite had been short. After the nurse, the doctor. An injection and comparative relief.

Levert had something he wanted to say, but was at a loss how to begin.

"I'm going to take advantage of a moment when you're not in pain to bring up a delicate subject. . . . I would have preferred not to. . . . This morning I received a visit from my colleague Jalibert. He knows of your . . . your accident. He is at your entire disposal. He offered to second me if necessary. . . . Finally, if you prefer a private hospital . . ."

"Thank you."

That was all. François had understood. But it didn't interest him. At that moment he was far away.

He was indeed an eminently practical man. Everybody was agreed on that. Some people even criticized

40

him for being too practical, for lacking imagination and sensitivity.

In only a few years, starting with his father's little tannery on the outskirts of the city, where the river-banks were nothing but grassy slopes haunted by fishermen, he had developed ten different enterprises, scattered throughout the department, employing hundreds of workers, men and women.

These enterprises were as different as possible, to all appearances, and their logical connection only he, perhaps, with Félix, understood: the tannery entailed buying hides in the country; the hides forced him to turn his attention to animals; to find a use for the casein, hitherto considered a waste product, he started a factory for the manufacture of plastics. People had been amazed at the goblets, salad forks and spoons, thimbles, and even powder boxes he turned out.

To have more casein, more milk had to be treated. He had brought a specialist from Holland, and a year later built a plant just outside the city, and began making Dutch cheese.

Cheese . . .

All this was done deliberately, without avidity, without ruthlessness, without ceasing to improve Chestnut Grove, without ceasing to enjoy life.

Yet suddenly, as now, while the doctor was talking of serious matters, François's mind would take flight.

It was not imagination; it was not poetic flight. He remained logical.

Félix had said, in speaking of Fachot, who had apparently been embarrassed:

"She put him at ease right away. . . ."

To him, the scene was much clearer than to Félix,

down to the smallest details, including the violet color of the moving shadows, for he knew the different aspects of Chestnut Grove at every hour of the day.

". . . at ease . . ."

That's how their own acquaintance had begun, with this aptitude of Bébé's. Chestnut Grove, with its heavy atmosphere of almost too prosperous countryside, disappeared and in its place he saw Royan: its immense white casino, its villas, the white sand dotted with bright bathing suits and multicolored umbrellas.

At the baccarat table, Madame d'Onneville, hardly less fat than now, in just as diaphanous a white dress and billowing tulle.

François knew nothing about her except that she was staying at the same hotel, the Royal, and that when she lost at baccarat she always looked suspiciously at the dealers, as though convinced that all their machinations were directed against her personally.

What was that little tart's name? Betty? Daisy? A dancer from Paris who appeared every night in one of the Royan clubs. She had wanted to try her luck. François handed her money, small amounts at a time.

"Hell! I'm tired of losing. Let's go get a drink at the bar . . . Coming?"

It was packed, as it always was around the fifteenth of August. Betty or Daisy had a shrill voice and dazzling beach pajamas.

"There are potato chips, I hope. . . . Barman! A Manhattan."

Félix was there at the bar too, with two young girls François seemed to recognize. A few moments later, he remembered: they were the daughters of the baccarat player in the diaphanous dress.

Félix, a little shy, was not sure if he should . . .

"Would you permit me to introduce my brother? . . . Mademoiselle Jeanne d'Onneville. Her sister, Mademoiselle . . . I'm sorry, I'm afraid I forgot your first name."

"I haven't any. Everybody calls me Bébé."

Those were the first words François heard her speak.

"Aren't you going to introduce me? . . . You're so polite!"

"This is a friend of mine, Mademoiselle Daisy [or Betty] . . ."

The crowd pressed the little group against the high mahogany bar. With a glance, Félix, looking a trifle sheepish, made his brother understand the situation: he was courting Jeanne d'Onneville, who was even then plump and good-natured.

"What if we go out on the pier? It's infernally hot in here!"

A situation both commonplace and ridiculous at the end of a sunny afternoon. Félix happened to walk in front with Jeanne. François followed with Daisy and the other young girl, Bébé, who was not yet eighteen. Daisy was soon bored. It was like walking with the family.

"Aren't we having a hell of a good time!"

"Look at the sun going to bed. Isn't that a diverting spectacle?" François said calmly.

"I can think of something more diverting in the way of going to bed. But if that's what you like . . ."

43

She had walked a few hundred yards more in sulky silence.

"I can't take any more of this! Enough's enough. . . . Bye!"

And with that she disappeared into the crowd.

"You mustn't mind her, mademoiselle."

"Why do you apologize? It's perfectly natural, isn't it?"

"Ah!"

She had understood. She was putting him at ease.

"Has your brother a girlfriend too?"

"Why do you ask?"

"Because I think he's serious about my sister."

She was more than slender at that time; her legs were long, her figure lithe, but nothing ever made her avert her glance. She would look straight at you without smiling, until it was really embarrassing.

"Tonight your girlfriend will make a scene. I hope you'll forgive me. It's because of your brother and my sister. You see, if I didn't stay with my sister, Mother would be furious."

She was right about the scene. And perhaps if it hadn't been for Daisy's remark:

"If you're going to start running after virgins now . . ."

Next day François began to look at Bébé differently, with a certain timidity. He became all the more awkward when he felt that she noticed the change in him. There was a suggestion of irony, and of satisfaction, in her eyes, and the way she responded to the pressure of his hand.

44

"Was your girlfriend very angry?"

"It doesn't matter in the least."

"Did you know that my sister and your brother not only see each other every day, but also write to each other? . . . Do you live in Paris?"

"No—the provinces."

"Ah! . . . We've always lived in Constantinople. . . . Until my father died. Now we're not going back to Turkey. Mother has a place in the Aube."

"Where?"

"At Maufrand. It's away from everything. . . . An old house that's been in the family. A sort of little manor house, which will have to be all done over."

"That's only fifteen kilometers from where I live," he told her.

Three months later, in the church at Maufrand, the two brothers married the two sisters. Bored in her big musty house, Madame d'Onneville moved to the city in the middle of the winter and reserved one day a week to spend at each of her daughters'.

And nothing of all this would have happened if, on the pier at Royan, Bébé had not put François at ease. She had not done it casually. From the moment they met at the bar of the casino, she had known perfectly well what she was doing. He was convinced of that.

A couple was walking in front of them, a couple who already seemed like a couple—Jeanne and Félix.

And what had she done, as soon as they were alone together, he and Bébé? Why, she too had changed her way of walking. There is a certain way of walking beside a man; there is a way, in talking to him, of turning to him and holding his eyes with yours.

There's something in the way bodies relax, even in the midst of a crowd.

Bébé had planned it. Hadn't she been a little put out when he said he didn't live in Paris?

She had wanted to be married, like her sister.

She had wanted to have a house of her own, her own servants . . .

That is what, for ten years, this clearheaded man believed. Did he hate her? The word is probably too strong. The fact is that he would often look at her, as she had looked at him at Royan, with critical eyes. And the first time he possessed her, he had no illusions.

Her flesh is flabby! he observed.

He didn't like her flesh. He didn't like her too-white skin, or her passive way of giving herself, of keeping her eyes open, their expression untroubled the whole time.

She had wanted to become Bébé Donge.

For ten years there had been no doubt in his mind about it. His attitude was simply the outcome of this certainty. He was a man who, once he had admitted a truth, accepted all the consequences that logically grew out of it.


"The examining magistrate telephoned me this morning to find out if he might question you."

François discovered the doctor standing by his bed again, shaking down a thermometer.

"I thought I was justified in saying you needed a few days' rest. The stomach pumpings have weakened you considerably. . . . He did not insist. As he said to me over the phone, so long as *she* admits her guilt."

The look his patient turned on him disturbed the doctor, making him wonder if he'd spoken out of turn. For Levert thought he saw, in François's eyes, frank astonishment at the word "guilt."

"Perhaps I should apologize for bringing up the subject. But I thought, considering our friendly relationship . . ."

"You are right, Doctor."

Exactly as with Sister Adonie, the doctor and other people were deceived by his calmness, by that almost blissful serenity that seemed to emanate from him at a time when everyone supposed him to be prey to terrible thoughts.

"I'll come back early in the afternoon. . . . After the shot I've just given you, you'll sleep for several hours."

François closed his eyes long before the doctor left him, felt vaguely that Sister was opening the window and pulling down the blind. He could hear birds singing. Sometimes a car crunched over one of the gravel drives. Patients were strolling about talking, but only an unintelligible murmur reached him. There came a faint tinkling of the chapel bells; then, probably at noon, the refectory bell's deeper tone.

He would have to keep a firm hold on his train of thought, go very far back, not forget anything, not omit the most insignificant detail.

But things kept intervening, preventing him from thinking: Jacques with the fish on his hook, the blinding sunlight on the red tennis court, the mushrooms

47

he had been sent to get in town, the striped awning of the Café du Centre, the little marble-topped tables with copper bands, and, in the shade . . .

When Jacques was born, in Dr. Pechin's hospital—before the doctor had retired and gone to live in the Midi—the atmosphere was about the same as that here at St. John's. In the morning they had made him wait in the garden, which was full of tulips, for it was April. He could hear the echoing bustle in the rooms and corridors. Windows were opening, and he sensed the end of the morning confusion, everything now in order for the day, fresh sheets, the breakfast trays removed, babies being brought back to their mothers.

The young mothers were sitting up in bed, the nurses scurrying from one room to another.

"You may come now, Monsieur Donge."

Just as when Félix had been brought to his room after waiting impatiently at the end of the corridor, no one had thought of the hours that had gone before. Everything was neat and clean. All trace of suffering had been carefully erased.

Bébé's anxious smile—for there had been anxiety in her smile! Why was he discovering only now that it was anxiety?

At the time, he had imagined that she was bitter because he was a man, because he hadn't suffered, because for him life went on as in the past, because before coming to see her, he had gone to his office, seen people about business. . . . Who knows? Perhaps because he had taken advantage of the freedom he had enjoyed on account of her—

Sister Adonie was tiptoeing around. She leaned over him, saw that he was quiet, thought he was asleep.

48

Isn't one always and inevitably wrong about what one thinks of others?

"Mother came yesterday. She insists that the baby is a Donge and has nothing of our family . . ."

What should he have said that he had not said?

"Clo doesn't look after you too badly? The house isn't too untidy?"

It was his father's house, next to the tannery, facing the river. He had had it modernized, but it had kept its old-fashioned air. There were unexpected hallways, walls that no architect had put there, rooms on different levels, cupolas . . .

"I always get lost in that old labyrinth!" Madame d'Onneville was constantly complaining, accustomed as she was to the modern apartment houses in Pera, with windows overlooking the Golden Horn. "I can't see why you don't build."

Félix and Jeanne lived a few streets away, in a somewhat more modern house, but Jeanne had no taste for housekeeping. Or for looking after her children. She liked to read and smoke in bed, she played bridge, and she was active on committees of various charity organizations, just for the pleasure of moving around.

"If I'm not back at eight, Félix, will you put the children to bed?"

And Félix would put the children to bed.

What was this uproar, this sudden hubbub of voices, exactly like people coming out of high mass Sunday mornings? It was visiting day. The doors had just been opened. Patients' families, with grapes and oranges and candy, were swarming through the corridors and the wards.

49

"Quiet, please! There's a very serious case in this room . . . sleeping. . . ."

Sister Adonie was mounting guard at the door of Number Six. Had François slept?

He had never seen the examining magistrate's office. He imagined it as dimly lighted by a lamp with a green shade on the desk. In one corner, a closet. Why a closet? He didn't know. He saw a closet and an enamel washbasin and a towel hanging on a hook.

He had once caught a glimpse of the man, appointed barely a month ago. Blond and insipid, rather fat and rather bald, with a rather horse-faced wife.

The defendants would be seated on rush-bottomed chairs. What dress would Bébé wear? The green dress she had on Sunday? Surely not. It was an afternoon dress, a dress for the country. He seemed to remember that it had been given the name Weekend.

Bébé would choose a tailored suit. She had a sense of fitness. When she was a young girl . . . But no, they could interrogate her all they liked, she would tell them nothing. She was incapable of talking about herself.

Modesty? Pride?

One day, when he happened to be angry, he had lashed out at her:

"You're just like your mother, who thinks she has to cut her name in two! Your whole family's eaten up with pride."

The Donnevilles . . . pardon me, d'Onnevilles . . . On the other side, the Donges, the two Donge brothers, sons of the tanner Donge, energetic, stubborn, who by dint of patience and willpower . . .

50

Even that first name, Bébé! . . . And that Turkish coffee they prepared in a trumpery copper service reminiscent of Constantinople.

Bazaars . . . showy rubbish . . . incense burners . . .

While they, the Donge brothers, were tanning hides, utilizing the casein, making cheese, and, for a year now, raising hogs, because there was enough waste matter to fatten them on.

Wasn't Chestnut Grove, the result of all this effort, and the silk stockings, dresses sent from Paris, and lingerie that . . . ?

And that enormous Madame d'Onneville, with her smug, idiotic pride, her scarfs, her hair dyed lavender, God knows how . . .

And Bébé, in bed, in sexual intercourse, was impossible. She endured it, that was all. After it, he felt like apologizing.

"Does it bore you?"

"Of course not!"

And with a sigh, she would go into the bathroom to efface all trace of their intimacy.

But if, fundamentally, François had been wrong —that is, about Royan—if she had not coldly made up her mind that he should marry her? If . . .

Then he would have to reconsider everything, revise everything. She would tell them nothing, and it wouldn't be through pride. It would be . . .


"Oh, poor man . . . But you were told to ring. Now look—your bed's covered with blood again."

51

He was sorry afterward, but it was too strong for him.

He looked at Sister Adonie as if she were a tree, a fence, anything but a good-hearted nun worrying about other people's welfare, physical and spiritual, and in a hard voice he snapped at her:

"What the devil is it to you?"

## — *4* —

Two cleaning women instead of one had made the room spick and span. The nurse had helped, and Sister Adonie, as excited as she would be over the visit of the bishop, had supervised everything in person.

"Put the table by the window . . . No, the chair on the other side. Otherwise *he* won't have a good light for writing. . . ."

All this for a paunchy, balding man, who finally arrived and hurried along the corridors with an embarrassed air, followed by a young man nattily dressed, like those who swarm the streets on Sunday.

"Yes, Sister . . . Thank you, Sister . . . Don't bother, Sister . . . This will do nicely, Sister. . . ."

He was Monsieur Giffre, the examining magistrate. Since he had come from Chartres, this was anything but an advancement. His political views were far to the right, and it was said that he had succeeded in getting a conviction against an influential member of the Grand Lodge. People made fun of him because of his beret and his bicycle, but especially because of his six children, whom he took walking solemnly and proudly, as though in a parade.

For a month after his arrival he had been unable to find suitable quarters. Finally a doctor who lived eight kilometers outside the city let him have a dilapidated old house without water or electricity but which contained a few odd pieces of furniture.

Had Monsieur Giffre perhaps seen François Donge on the street? Surely he had heard of him. But the two men had never been introduced to each other.

On entering the room, he simply bowed and took four quick steps toward the little table made ready for him by the window. Opening his briefcase, and while his clerk was getting out his notebook, he spoke:

"Doctor Levert tells me that I can have about half an hour. Of course, I will leave the moment you feel the least fatigue. Now, with your permission, I will begin. Your name?"

"François-Charles-Emile Donge, son of Charles-Hubert-Chrétien Donge, tanner, deceased; and of Emilie-Hortense Fillâtre, no profession, deceased."

"Have you ever been convicted of a crime?"

He mumbled this hurriedly, with a wave of his hand, as if brushing away a fly, and gave a little cough. He had not yet looked toward the bed where François lay propped up by several pillows. From the other side of the window (the shade had been pulled down and formed a large golden rectangle), the slow footsteps of the patients could be heard on the gravel as they took their daily exercise.

54

"Sunday, the twentieth of August, while you were at your country house, Chestnut Grove, in the district of Ornaie, an attempt was made to poison you."

Silence. The magistrate raised his eyes and saw François looking at him attentively.

"You agree?"

"I don't know."

"Doctor Pinaud, who was called in, declares that no doubt is possible, and that about two o'clock in the afternoon of that day you swallowed a large dose of arsenic, probably in your coffee."

Again silence.

"Do you deny these facts?"

"I was very sick, that I admit."

"In other words, you refuse to bring an action? . . . I must tell you that under the circumstances we are forced to bring charges, even with no action on the victim's part."

François said nothing. He looked at the examining magistrate the way he always looked at people. How could this man, with so much on his mind—his children, his makeshift living quarters, those eight kilometers he would have to cover on his bicycle before lunch, the intrigues that had already begun around him—how could he hope to discover, merely by opening a dossier, the least particle of truth about Bébé Donge, when her own husband, who had lived with her ten years . . . ?

"And now, although it is not strictly regular, I am going to read you the report of Madame Donge's first questioning. Or more exactly her declaration made to Sergeant Janvier, Sunday, August 20, at five o'clock.

*"I, Eugénie-Blanche-Clémentine, age twenty-seven, wife of François Donge, declare under oath, the following: Today, being at Chestnut Grove, which belongs to my husband and his brother in common, I tried to poison my husband, François Donge, by putting arsenic in his coffee.*

*"I have nothing more to say."*

The examining magistrate raised his eyes just in time to see a smile flit over François's lips.

"You see, your wife acknowledges the facts."

Rarely had Monsieur Giffre felt as he did now, facing this sickbed, that he was prying into something that was none of his business. Even in front of Madame Donge . . .

"I will now read you the transcript of the questioning of the defendant I conducted yesterday."

He regretted the word "defendant," but it was too late, and François winced. At the questioning, he wondered, had Bébé worn a dress or a suit? Before hearing the words she had spoken, he felt the need to visualize her in a definite setting. He half closed his eyes and without an effort saw the pier at Royan and, from behind, the couple that Félix and Jeanne formed.

"I'll spare you the usual formalities and read you only the principal questions and answers.

"Question: *Just when did you decide to attempt to take your husband's life?*

"Answer: *I don't know exactly.*

"Question: *Several days before the attempt? Several months?*

"Answer: *Several months, probably.*

56

"Question: *Why do you say* probably?

"Answer: *Because it was a rather vague idea.*

"Question: *What do you mean by 'a rather vague idea'?*

"Answer: *I felt, in a confused way, that we would come to that in the end, but I wasn't sure.*"

François gave a sigh. The examining magistrate glanced up at him, but it was too late. François's face showed nothing but scrupulous attention.

"Shall I continue? I'm not tiring you?"

"Not at all."

"Then I'll resume:

"*. . . but I wasn't sure.*

"Question: *What do you mean by the words 'that we would come to that'? You use the plural. I don't understand.*

"Answer: *I don't either.*

"Question: *Had the misunderstanding between you been going on for a long time?*

"Answer: *There has never been any misunderstanding between my husband and me.*

"Question: *Then what grievance have you against him?*

"Answer: *I have no grievance against him.*

"Question: *Have you any reason to be jealous?*

"Answer: *I have no idea, but I am not jealous.*

"Question: *If we cannot attribute your act to jealousy, what was your motive?*

"Answer: *I don't know.*

"Question: *In your family, has there ever been any case of mental illness? What did your father die of?*

"Answer: *Amebic dysentery.*

"Question: *And your mother is sound in body and mind? Doctor Bollanger, who examined you from this point of view, affirms that you are responsible for your actions. What was the nature of your relationship with your husband?*

57

"Answer: *We lived together under the same roof, and we have a son.*

"Question: *Did frequent quarrels occur?*

"Answer: *Never.*

"Question: *From any indications, do you think that your husband had an outside attachment?*

"Answer: *I never thought about it.*

"Question: *If that had been the case, would you have sought revenge in one way or another?*

"Answer: *It would not have affected me.*

"Question: *In short, you say that for several months you have been more or less sure that you were going to kill your husband, but that you do not know your reason for so drastic a decision?*

"Answer: *Exactly.*

"Question: *Where and when did you obtain the poison?*

"Answer: *I cannot tell you the precise date, but it was sometime in May.*

"Question: *That is, three months before the crime? Continue.*

"Answer: *I had gone into town to buy various things, perfume among others.*

"Question: *One moment. Do you live at Chestnut Grove most of the time?*

"Answer: *For the last three years, almost all the time, because of my son's health. Although he's not really ill, he is delicate and needs fresh air.*

"Question: *Does your husband live at Chestnut Grove with you?*

"Answer: *Not all the time. He comes out for two, sometimes for three, days a week. He may arrive in the evening and go back the next morning.*

58

"Question: *Thank you. Continue. You had got as far as a certain day in May. . . .*

"Answer: *It was toward the middle of the month, I remember. . . . I had not taken enough money with me, so I went to the tannery.*

"Question: *To your husband's tannery? Did you go there often?*

"Answer: *No, hardly ever. His business affairs didn't interest me. . . . He was not in his office. I went to the laboratory, thinking he might be there. My husband is a chemist and does experiments. . . . In a little glass cabinet I saw several bottles with labels. . . .*

"Question: *Until that day you had never thought of poison?*

"Answer: *I don't think so. The word 'arsenic' struck me. . . . I took the bottle, which had a little grayish-white powder left in it, and put it in my bag.*

"Question: *At that moment you conceived the idea of using it?*

"Answer: *Perhaps . . . It's difficult to say. . . . My husband came in and gave me some money.*

"Question: *Did you have to account to him for the money you spent?*

"Answer: *He has always given me all the money I wanted.*

"Question: *And so, for three months you hid the poison, waiting for the moment to use it. What made you choose that Sunday, rather than some other day?*

"Answer: *I don't know. . . . I'm getting rather tired, and if you don't mind . . .*"

Monsieur Giffre raised his head. He was embarrassed. He looked like he might run his fingers through his skimpy hair.

"That is all I succeeded in eliciting. I am hoping that you might be able to enlighten me further."

Forgetting his official position, he looked at François Donge man to man. Then he rose, to pace up and down the little whitewashed room, his hands thrust deep into the pockets of his somewhat baggy trousers.

"I hardly need tell you, Monsieur Donge, that everybody in town is talking of a crime of passion, and that certain names have been mentioned. . . . I know that this gossip can have no effect on justice. But have you noticed anything to lead you to suppose that your wife knew about any affair you might have had?"

With what haste he spoke! And how abruptly he stopped pacing, dumbfounded by François's reply:

"My wife knew about all my affairs with women."

"You mean to say you told her?"

"If she asked me."

"You must excuse me for insisting. It is so surprising that I feel the need of further clarification. . . . So you had not one, but numerous love affairs? . . ."

"Quite a few . . . Most of them brief and of no consequence."

"And when you came home, you would tell your wife . . . ?"

"I looked upon her as a friend. She put me at ease."

The phrase struck François, and he grew thoughtful.

"Have these confidences been going on for long?"

"Several years . . . I can't say just how long."

60

"But you remained husband and wife? . . . I mean you still had normal marital relations?"

"Not very often . . . My wife's health, especially since her confinement, prevented . . ."

"I understand. She allowed you to seek elsewhere what she couldn't give you."

"Something like that, although not exactly."

"You never sensed in her the least jealousy?"

"Not the least."

"To the very end, that is until Sunday, you were good friends?"

Slowly François looked at the magistrate, from head to toe. He saw him in the midst of his family, in the doctor's dilapidated house, which he knew. He saw him on the road on his bicycle, with clips around his trousers. He saw him Sundays walking to high mass, followed by his six children and his careworn wife.

Hardly moving his lips, he said, "Yes." The clerk kept diligently writing, with the sunlight, filtering through the shade, reflected on his well-oiled hair.

"Allow me to stress this point, Monsieur Donge."

And the examining magistrate threw him the humble glance of a man who knows very well that he ought not to insist, but who is only doing his duty.

"I assure you that I have nothing more to tell you, Monsieur Giffre."

That "Monsieur Giffre" was so unexpected that they looked at each other as though they were no longer an examining magistrate and a witness, but two men placed in an awkward situation. The examining magistrate coughed and turned to his clerk, as though to tell him to omit the "Monsieur Giffre," but the clerk did not need to be told.

"I am anxious to turn the dossier over to the public prosecutor as soon as possible, in order to allay all the excitement that affairs of this sort invariably stir up in a small town."

"Has my wife chosen a lawyer?"

"At first she refused to have a lawyer. At my insistence, she finally chose Maître Boniface."

The best lawyer at the local bar, a man of about sixty, bearded and self-important, whose fame was not only local but radiated through several departments.

"He saw his client yesterday afternoon. From what I gathered, when he came to see me afterward, he made no more headway than I had."

So much the better! After all, what business was it of theirs? What were these two men so bent on discovering? And what could they do with the truth if, by a miracle, they found it?

The truth! . . .

"Listen, your honor . . ."

No! It was too soon. The time was not yet ripe.

"Yes, I'm listening."

"Forgive me . . . I forget what I was going to say. . . . You very kindly told me that if I felt tired . . ."

It wasn't true. His mind had never been more alert. This conversation had done him good. He had engaged in a kind of mental gymnastics, which had swept away the cobwebs.

"I understand. We will leave you. . . . I beg you to think it over, however, and I'm sure you will see that it is your duty, and in the interest of your wife, as well as in the interest of justice . . ."

Of course, your honor! You are a very worthy man, a model citizen, an admirable husband and father, an incorruptible, even intelligent magistrate. When I leave the hospital, I must help you find a charming little house, for I know the city better than anyone, and I have a good deal of influence. You see, I bear you no grudge, I understand your position.

Only don't, for heaven's sake, touch Bébé Donge. Don't try to understand Bébé Donge.

"With my apologies for having tired you . . ."

"Not at all . . . Not at all . . ."

"I wish you good day."

He bowed and left the room, and in the corridor he found Sister Adonie waiting to escort him to the glass-paneled entrance door. His clerk followed, dazzled by the sunlight.

And François, sitting up in bed, staring at the table, which had been of so little use, said to himself that Bébé had behaved exactly as she should have behaved.

Never, in fact, had he felt closer to her. Some of the answers she gave, he himself might have prompted them. At times, while the examining magistrate was reading, he'd felt like nodding with approval.

Was he happy? He did not ask himself that question, but he felt lighthearted, satisfied.

"It is kind of you, Sister. . . . Yes, please open the window. I begin to like this shady courtyard and the patients with their slow-motion walk. . . . Yesterday, I saw one, an old man, who was hiding behind a tree, smoking."

63

"Hush! If you tell me who it was, I'll be obliged to punish him."

"What would you do?"

"I'd have to take away his 'Sunday.' You see, we give the old men in the hospital, who haven't much chance of getting out, a little pin money on Sunday."

"For tobacco, you mean?"

His eyes were twinkling.

"My wallet must be in one of my coat pockets. Take whatever you find there . . . for your old men's 'Sunday.' "

"Oh! I forgot. You have a visitor. But I wonder . . ."

"I swear, Sister, I'm not a bit tired. Who is it?"

"Doctor Jalibert."

Naturally! The good sister, too, had heard the gossip. It was plain from her air of shocked modesty.

"Let him come in, Sister. He must be very worried."

"He's been pacing up and down in the corridor for half an hour, smoking the whole time. . . . I didn't dare say anything, because he's a doctor, but . . ."

Jalibert came rushing into the room wearing a fixed smile.

"How are you, old man? . . . It wasn't too bad, I hope. Levert says you've stood it very well."

Sister Adonie left the room with disapproval written all over her.

"I ran into the examining magistrate just now. . . . I happened to be seeing one of my patients in the hospital. . . . I wouldn't have bothered you if they hadn't told me you were quite all right this morning. Do you mind if I . . ."

64

He lighted a cigarette, began pacing, stopped short, started again, went over to the window. He was thin, unattractive in body and soul.

"I suppose poor old Giffre—between ourselves, he isn't exactly a genius and hasn't much of a reputation around here—tried to worm things out of you?"

"He was extremely correct."

"Discreet?" asked Jalibert with an uncertain smile.

"He is doing his best to discover the truth—a truth I myself still don't know."

And Jalibert, crudely:

"You're joking!"

To think that because of Olga Jalibert, who had a body as firm and succulent as a plum and who threw herself into love as into life, with insolent ardor, François had had to shake hands with this man dozens of times, play bridge with him, and eat at his table!

"After all, you must know by now what your wife's defense will be. . . . Seems she's retained Boniface. . . . I can't quite see that stuffed shirt pleading a case like this."

He must have been worried sick. He was waiting for a word from François, just one, but François, to tease him, put off saying it.

What else would Jalibert come up with to try to force him to speak?

"Boniface, with that square beard of his, those bushy eyebrows and shiny robe, poses as a plaster saint. He's a man who wouldn't hesitate, for the sake of a spectacular defense and in the name of morality, to bring disgrace on an entire community. . . . To entrust an affair of passion to a lawyer like that, it's . . ."

65

Relenting, François said very quietly:

"There's no question of an affair of passion."

The other man had to make an effort not to leap for joy, to try simply to look astonished.

"Then what is your wife's defense going to be?"

"She is not making any defense."

"Does she deny it? The paper this morning said . . ."

"What did it say?"

"That she has confessed everything, including premeditation."

"That's true."

"So?"

"So nothing!"

Jalibert, who himself would have killed ten patients to enlarge his hospital or to buy a better car, couldn't believe his ears. He looked at François uneasily, suspiciously.

"But she'll *have* to enter a defense. And in doing that, she may involve a third party."

"She will enter no defense."

"She was always a hard woman to understand," said Jalibert, with a wry smile. "I was talking about her yesterday—I don't remember with whom. I said . . ."

"No one has ever been able to figure out what Bébé thinks."

"It might be her education in Constantinople. . . . You must admit that her mother is odd enough herself. . . . But what motive does she give for her act?"

"She doesn't give any."

"Is she pleading insanity? You know, medically, it's perfectly tenable, and, as far as I'm concerned, if any testimony is required . . . I spoke to Levert on the subject. He would sign a certificate if necessary. . . . Tell me . . ."

François made an effort not to smile as he looked at him.

"If you could get at Boniface, or, since that would be a little irregular, get someone you can trust to approach him . . . If he pleads insanity, he's sure of winning his case, and I, for my part, will take care of the doctors appointed by the court."

"Bébé is not insane. Don't worry, Jalibert. You'll see: everything will be all right. . . . How's the work coming? Have they started the pavilion yet? . . . Now you must forgive me, but it's time for my treatment. . . ."

He stretched out his arm and rang. Sister Adonie knocked soundlessly at the door and entered without waiting for an answer.

"Did you call?"

"They can begin the treatment, Sister. If the nurse is free . . ."

He was in a hurry to have it over with, so that he could be alone in his room, all neat and clean, the window open on the courtyard, the sheets fresh and cool, his body empty, and his mind torpid from the hypodermic he received twice a day.

He was in such a hurry to find Bébé again that he did not wait for Jalibert to leave. He hardly heard him say good-by. His eyes were closed. He felt himself being undressed, turned, he felt hands on him. . . .

"Am I hurting you?"

He didn't reply. He was far away. It did hurt, but he didn't mind.

67

. . . A hotel room, a resort hotel, with bay windows and a dazzling white balcony from which one could see, on the other side of the Croisette, the entire harbor of Cannes, its tangle of masts, long slim hulls almost touching each other, and the lavender-blue immensity filled with the chug-chug of power-boats . . .

Félix and Jeanne had chosen Naples. It was only for the sake of appearance, "what people might think," that the two brothers had separated for their honeymoons. Who knows, after all, if it hadn't been a mistake?

A night journey in a sleeper. A station smothered in mimosa. The hotel barker waiting for them.

"Monsieur and Madame Donge? . . . This way, please . . ."

François was wearing his most ironic smile, looking the way he always looked when he wasn't pleased with himself. In fact, he was panicky, and felt ridiculous besides. Isn't it a ridiculous role, that of young bridegroom, with the compartment still full of flowers, presents brought to you at the last moment, and this young girl waiting to be made a woman, knowing that the moment is imminent, probably watching you surreptitiously, with a mixture of impatience and fear?

"Do you know, François, what I'd like to do?"

They were still saying *vous*. In fact, after ten years of marriage, they often reverted to it.

"I'm afraid you'll think I'm silly. . . . I feel like going rowing. . . . It will remind me of the Bosporus. . . . Do you mind?"

No! Yes! . . . It was really too preposterous. And

it became even more preposterous when they couldn't find a rowboat. The quays were lined with motorboats, whose owners clamored for customers.

"A ride on the water . . . To the Iles Ste-Marguerite?"

Bébé, insensible to ridicule, clung to his arm, whispering:

"A little boat just for the two of us . . ."

They finally succeeded in finding a rowboat. It was heavy. The oars were poorly attached and kept coming out of the oarlocks. It was hot. Bébé, on the stern seat, sat dabbling her hands in the water, just like a pretty picture. Fishermen looked at them and grinned. They were nearly run down by an incoming yacht.

"Are you angry? . . . Sometimes, on the Bosporus, I used to go out in a *yali* all alone, and I'd let myself drift with the current until it was almost completely dark. . . ."

Yes, naturally! On the Bosporus! . . .

"If you're tired, let's go back."

He felt like having a drink at the bar, but she was already in the elevator. Even the elevator boy had a knowing grin. It was ten o'clock in the morning.

"Doesn't all this light frighten you, François? I feel as if the sea were looking at us!"

The sea looking . . .

He pulled down the blinds. And everything was cut into thin slices, including Bébé's body.

She didn't know how to kiss. Her lips remained inert. As if the contact of lips seemed to her a barbarous necessity.

The whole time, she lay there with her eyes open, gazing at the ceiling, and now and then across her pale face would come a twitch, as though of pain.

What was it he had said exactly? Something like:

"You'll see later, in a few days . . ."

She had squeezed his hand with her moist fingers, murmuring:

"Of course, François . . ."

The way one speaks to please someone, so he won't be too unhappy. Her little breasts, which were not exactly flabby, but not firm either, and the hollows on either side of her neck . . .

Not knowing what to do, he got up and went over to the bay window. He raised the blinds, lighted a cigarette. What he really wanted to do was ring for a whiskey or a glass of port. The sun was shining on the bed. Bébé had pulled the covers over her. As her head was buried in the pillows, he could see nothing but her fair hair. Because of certain tremors, he thought:

Is she crying?

He asked, using *tu* for the first time, in a tone that was both protective and ill-tempered. He had a horror of tears, a horror of everything that complicated simple healthy things, a horror of their ridiculous excursion in the rowboat, of those eyes staring at the ceiling, and now these tears.

"Listen, dear, I'll let you rest now. Come down in an hour or two, and we'll have lunch on the terrace."

When she came down, wearing a cream-colored dress with ruffles that was very young-wife and girlish at the same time, she seemed thinner than ever, more serious too, in the expression of her face and in her

70

movements. She forced herself to smile as she found him at the bar, where he had just ordered a cocktail.

"Oh, you're here!" she said.

Why, in those three words, did he sense a reproach? Why that glance at his cigarette?

"I was waiting for you. . . . Did you sleep?"

"I don't know."

The maître d' hovered respectfully.

"Would madame like to have lunch served in the sun or the shade?"

"In the sun," she replied.

Then quickly:

"But if you'd rather not, François . . ."

He preferred the shade, but said nothing.

"I disappointed you."

"Of course not."

"I'm sorry."

"Why do you insist on talking about it?"

He raised his head from the variety of hors d'oeuvres he was eating with a good appetite.

"I'm not hungry. But that mustn't stop you. . . . Only don't make me eat . . . You're angry, aren't you?"

What more?

"Of course I'm not angry!"

In spite of himself, his voice sounded furious.


"It's all over, Monsieur Donge. I hope it wasn't too painful? . . . Now you can rest for two or three hours. . . . Just a moment; you still have to have your injection."

Through the bars of his closing eyelashes, he caught a vague glimpse of the big white cap and the plump kindly face of Sister Adonie.

71

# — 5 —

He finished tying his tie without the help of a mirror. (Is it in order not to terrify the patients that there are never any mirrors in hospital rooms?) The window was wide open; the shade under the plane trees looked invitingly cool. In spite of the old men in blue sitting on the benches, in spite of the furtive passage of a stretcher, it was, he felt as he turned back to the room, a little sad to think that he could no longer be a part of all this. Even his sheets had been taken away that morning!

Félix, who had instinctively put on a light-colored suit that morning, came cheerfully out of the office, putting his wallet back into his pocket.

"Ready?"

"Ready. Is everything settled? . . . You didn't forget the nurses?"

François, no matter what the circumstances, never

forgot anything. The proof was that, his toilet kit in his hand, he now remarked, frowning:

"I should have told you not to give anything to the little cross-eyed brunette. . . . She ignored my call one night because it was time for her to go off duty."

They were walking along the corridor, which was paved with yellow tiles.

"Well, Sister Adonie! This time I'm leaving you! . . . By the way, we have a little matter to settle. You remember when I asked you to take money from my wallet? Why didn't you do it?"

"I didn't feel . . ."

"How many old men live here?"

"About twenty."

"Wait a moment . . . At ten francs a Sunday . . . Félix, give Sister Adonie a thousand francs, and you'll send her the same amount every month. On condition, Sister, that you close your eyes when you find tobacco in their pockets . . . That's understood, isn't it?"

Félix's car. The smell of the street, which had become unfamiliar to him.

"I see you fixed the fender."

"By the way . . ."

Félix, as he drove, spoke cautiously, now and then stealing a glance at his brother.

"Jeanne went to see *her* yesterday."

"What did she say?"

"She asked about Jacques. When she found out that Jeanne was looking after the boy with Marthe, she didn't seem to like it."

" 'I left Marthe detailed instructions,' she said. 'I wish *she'd* come to see me. . . .' But she was absolutely calm, exactly the same. 'Is Mother at Madame Ber-thollat's?' she asked."

"Look out!" cried François, grabbing the steering wheel. Félix, intent on his report, had just missed sideswiping a cart.

"Before she left, Jeanne said: 'Listen, Bébé. To me, at least, you can admit . . .' And your wife replied: 'To you less than to anyone, dear. Haven't you ever realized that we have nothing in common? Tell Marthe to come see me. . . . And don't look after Jacques.' "

It was ten in the morning. They kept passing big delivery vans. A fleeting glimpse of the marketplace.

"That's all?"

"Yes . . . At Chestnut Grove, everything's fine. . . . Naturally, Jeanne isn't too pleased. Especially about Jacques. She might as well have been told she wasn't competent to take care of children. . . . Of course, I know . . . Am I tiring you?"

"No."

Quai des Tanneurs, with the white house at the far end, and the uneven paving stones, on which François had played marbles as a boy. He got out of the car alone and entered the building, not by the private door to the house but through the office entrance.

"Good morning, Monsieur François!"

"Good morning, Madame Flament."

He had completely forgotten her existence! She was flushed and trembling, with one hand on her fluttering heart, and she gazed at him with great moist eyes. She had certainly been responsible for the roses on his desk.

"You can't imagine how horrified everybody was

74

when the news reached us! . . . You don't feel too weak?"

He turned his back on her and shrugged. The odor was there to greet him, the stale odor of the whole house, but of his office in particular, which was like no other odor in the world. The sun had a certain way of filtering between the crossbars of the low windows and shining on the polished furniture. There was one of these reflections on the wall just under the black-and-gold Louis-Philippe clock, a tremulous little disk which used to fascinate him as a child. In the afternoon, it moved to another wall and wandered over the framed photograph of the Congress of Master Tanners in Paris, in which his father stood with folded arms.

"Has Grand Bazaar of Nancy paid yet, Félix?"

"It's been a struggle, but they've finally done it."

This was the only room in the house that hadn't changed. The Donge brothers had modern offices elsewhere, but this one, here in the paternal house, was the hub of all their enterprises. The walls were hung with striped paper, turning yellow. François's desk, which had been his father's, had an inlaid top of dark green leather, stained with spots of violet ink, and pigeonholes above.

On the wall facing him he had hung the enlarged photograph of his father with long walrus mustache, thick hair, and the stiff white collar and black tie of an artisan dressed up for Sunday. Formerly, the portrait, with that of his mother, had hung in his bedroom. When Bébé came to live in the house and talked of modernizing it . . .

His mother was also in the office, on the other wall,

facing Félix's desk. Rush-bottomed chairs that François had known all his life . . .

Another odor . . . He was sitting there absently,
slowly taking possession of his home once more, of
his own quarters, soaking up the atmosphere, and
suddenly that odor . . .

"I put a personal letter for you on your desk."

Madame Flament, of course! He had forgotten the
odor of his secretary, a voluptuous redhead with
bright eyes, a ripe mouth, a well-filled blouse, and a
superb behind, who perspired freely.

Wasn't it because of her that, at the very beginning . . . ?

The letter, which came from Deauville, was in Olga
Jalibert's handwriting, and he was in no hurry to open
it. Félix, at his own desk, was going over the morning
mail.

Another morning, about two months after their
marriage, Bébé, in a light silk dress, had come to the
office unexpectedly.

"May I come in?"

Félix had gone out. Madame Flament was at her
desk. She had risen precipitously to bow, and had
started toward the door.

"Where are you going?" François had asked.

"I thought . . ."

"You don't need to go. What is it, dear?"

Bébé, not familiar with the office, was taking in all
the details.

"I just dropped in to say hello. . . . Ah! This is
where you put the portraits."

He noticed her wince as she passed the secretary:
the odor, of course.

At noon, while they were having lunch at the round dining-room table, she had asked:

"Does that girl have to stay in your office?"

"Madame Flament's a married woman. . . . She's been my secretary for six years. She's familiar with our businesses."

"I don't see how you can stand her odor."

Perhaps a great part of the trouble came from the idea rooted in him that his wife never did anything without some design. She spoke too calmly, looking straight into his eyes, as in Royan. Now she irritated him by saying in conclusion:

"But, after all, you know better than I what you have to do."

"True!"

What happened later proved she had some design in her head . . . And yet? Now, after all these years, he found himself wondering . . . Two or three times she got Félix to take her around the premises. . . . One Sunday morning a few days after, when, alone in his office, he was finishing some urgent business, she had come in, wearing a pale chiffon dress.

"Am I disturbing you?"

She wandered about the room. Sometimes he caught a glint from her lacquered fingernails, which she spent half an hour manicuring every morning.

"Tell me, François . . ."

"Yes?"

"Don't you think I could help you too?"

He looked at her, frowning.

"What would you want to do?"

"Work in the office here with you . . ."

"Instead of Madame Flament?"

77

"Why not? If you're worried about my typing, I'll pick it up again quickly. In Constantinople, I had a portable typewriter. I used to type all my letters for fun and . . ."

With her long red nails, of course, and her dresses as fragile as a butterfly's wing! She would come down at ten or eleven o'clock in an aroma of bath salts and beauty creams. . . .

So that was it! She was jealous of Madame Flament!

"It's impossible, dear. It would take you years to learn all the intricacies of the business. Besides, it isn't your place."

"I'm sorry. . . . I won't mention it again."

He might have added a few agreeable words to make her happy, but he had not done so. When, a little stiff, she was going out the door, he had almost risen to call her back.

No! He mustn't indulge such childishness, or life would be impossible.

A quarter of an hour later, he heard her walking about in their bedroom. What was she doing? Taking measurements probably. Matching fabrics. She was busy modernizing part of the house at that time. The photographs of his mother and father had already been taken down. Every evening she would spread out catalogues and samples.

"What do you think, François? This silk is very expensive, but I can't find anything else in this shade of green."

A faded almond green, her favorite color.

"Get it if you like . . . You know it doesn't make any difference to me."

"I'd rather have your opinion."

His opinion! Well, his opinion was that it would have been better to leave the house as it was. Had he made a mistake not to tell her so plainly? Perhaps. But he had let her amuse herself like a child, and during that time he was left in peace.

He didn't like to see her think. When she did, it was sometimes difficult to follow her. Besides, he had a horror of complications, and she complicated everything for no apparent reason.

For example, he remembered the second or third week after their return from Cannes. None of the old furnishings had yet been changed. They were still sleeping in his parents' big walnut bed; the same flowered paper was on the walls.

One morning, very early, while a rooster was crowing in a neighboring courtyard, François woke with the feeling that something was different. Uneasy, he lay motionless for a moment. Then he opened his eyes and saw Bébé sitting up in bed beside him, watching him intently:

"What are you doing?"

"Nothing . . . I was listening to your breathing. It's louder when you lie on your left side than when you're on your right."

It wasn't exactly the thing to put him in a good humor.

"I've always slept badly on my left side."

"Do you know what I was thinking, François? That from now on we will always live together, that we'll grow old together and die together."

She looked somber, and so very thin in her nightdress, and he wanted only to go back to sleep. It was barely five in the morning.

"I've been thinking, too, how I wish I had known your father."

It was a good thing she hadn't, considering the way old man Donge would have received a daughter-in-law like Bébé. Didn't she realize that? Hadn't she seen the photograph of the tanner, with his great mustache and arms fiercely folded, the way they were in all his photographs?

"Are you asleep?"

"No."

"Am I bothering you?"

"No."

"I'd like to ask you something else . . . to promise me something. . . . But you mustn't do it if you don't mean it. Promise me, no matter what happens, that you will always be frank with me. Promise always to tell the truth, even if you think it will hurt me. . . . You understand, François? . . . It would be too horrible to live all our life together, side by side, in an atmosphere of deceit. If you're disappointed, you must say so. If one day you don't love me any longer, you must tell me that too, and we'll each go our own way. . . . If you're unfaithful to me, I won't be angry, but I want to know. . . . You promise?"

"You have strange ideas in the morning."

"I've been thinking about it a long time . . . ever since we were married. You don't want to promise?"

"Of course I will."

"Look me in the eyes . . . so I'll feel it's a real promise and that I can count on you."

"I promise. Now, go to sleep."

She may not have gone to sleep right away, but at

ten the next morning she was still sleeping, more serenely than usual.


"Madame Flament!"

"Yes, Monsieur Donge?"

"Get the superintendent . . . Tell him to put your desk in the next room."

"The storeroom?"

"He can move his pails and brooms somewhere else. There's room for them in the shed at the back of the courtyard."

He saw her lower lip poke out. He looked down at the flowers on his desk, and when he looked up again, his eyes were colder.

"Right away?"

"Right away."

"Have I done something wrong?"

It was at moments like this, without raising his voice, almost without a change of expression, his pupils strangely transparent, that he was the most terrifying.

"I didn't say you did anything wrong. Go get the superintendent, and tell him to hurry."

He went to the window and leaned his forehead against the glass, seeing the quay with the eyes of his childhood.

After all this time, it was impossible to say in exactly what order these things had happened: first, the scene in bed and the strange promise; then, Madame Flament and her odor. Next, that crazy idea of working in the office as his secretary . . .

81

She wasn't jealous of women only; she was jealous of his work, of everything in and about him that didn't include her.

Even her regretting not having known old man Donge! Why, in heaven's name? To get to know the family tree better?

What else was it she said, a few weeks later? No, it was at least two months, even three months later, since Jeanne had just announced with charming casualness that she was going to have a baby.

"And to think I counted on marriage to get back my figure!" Jeanne said laughingly. "What's more, Mother's furious."

But Félix was happy. Nothing complicated his life. His mother-in-law had a weakness for him, whereas she always looked upon François with a certain misgiving.

One autumn evening, François and Bébé were strolling along the quay in front of the house. Their neighbors, in couples or in groups, were doing the same. The sun had set. Ever since he could remember, François had always seen his neighbors on the quay, taking the air along the river before going to bed.

After a long silence, Bébé, her hand resting on her husband's arm, had sighed.

"You're not angry with me?"

"For what?"

"What I asked you . . ."

"What did you ask me?"

Strangely, he thought it was about Madame Flament, and this, once more, put him in a bad humor.

"Don't you remember? . . . To wait two or three years before . . ."

And Bébé, always so precise, so self-possessed, faltered. At such moments she was a little girl again.

"Before having a baby? Is that it?"

Was *that* all?

"Yes, darling. I must explain. . . . It isn't that I'm selfish and just want to enjoy these years. . . . But I'm afraid, François."

"Afraid of what?"

"It seems to me that afterward it will never be the same again. . . . But if you'd rather not wait, if you want to have one sooner . . ."

He had squeezed her fingers with real tenderness. "Poor child . . ."

She was imagining things. After all, although he wanted children, he was in no particular hurry.

"You'll give me two more years?"

You'll give me! Was he, then, God the Father! Oh, well . . .

"Of course. Two years, four years . . . as many as you please. What's the matter?"

"I think it's beginning to get chilly."

"You never have anything on."

"I'm sorry."

It was true. She knew that in the evening it was chilly by the water. She knew that he liked this hour of relaxation, this stroll along the quay. Why then did she dress so absurdly, in a dress like a spiderweb and with nothing around her shoulders but a bit of silk without any warmth to it?

Another crotchet of hers was that now, whenever she had occasion to come to his office, either to ask him for money or for any other reason, she always knocked first. Madame Flament had noticed it and would give François a little knowing glance.

It was all the more ridiculous, considering that . . .

And the rest had occurred so stupidly. It was one winter night. They went to the theater to see a stock company in town for a short run. Madame d'Onneville, Félix, and Jeanne were there too. Afterward they lingered for some time at the Café du Centre. François and Bébé walked home, their footsteps echoing on the sidewalk.

At the corner near the bridge, they passed a couple glued against the wall in so close an embrace that they seemed to have only one body.

Bébé leaned more heavily on her husband's arm. Some distance farther along, about a hundred feet from their house, he felt the whole weight of her body against him, and he took her in his arms and kissed her tenderly.

To his surprise, she wrenched herself away and was suddenly cold and aloof.

"What's wrong?"

"Nothing."

"But, darling, a moment ago . . ."

She walked on quickly, waited for him to open the door, then rushed upstairs.

"You don't want to tell me what it is?"

A quick, sharp glance.

"You refuse?"

He took off his coat to make himself comfortable.

"Listen, François; you remember the promise you gave me one morning? . . . To tell me everything, no matter what happened? . . . Are you ready to keep it?"

He was suddenly seized with profound uneasiness.

84

"I don't understand. . . ."

"Why do you lie? . . . We agreed, didn't we, there would be no lies between us?"

She seemed very calm, very self-possessed.

"You really don't know why I pushed you away just now when you kissed me? . . . Take your coat . . . You didn't have time to change it before going to the theater."

He never dreamed at that moment that their whole life together was at stake. He was seated on the edge of the bed, thinking, weighing alternatives, watching Bébé and admiring her sangfroid.

"I told you I'm not jealous. . . . What I don't want . . . Do you understand? . . . Afterward I'll be your wife just as before, since I am your wife. . . . And you'll be able to tell me everything, the way you would tell a friend, the way you would tell Félix."

He stared at the silver-colored radiator that had just been installed. He had only a few seconds to make a vital decision.

"Has Madame Flament been your mistress for a long time?"

He passed his hand over his forehead, roughed up his hair, rose, and remained standing motionless in the middle of the room.

"Answer me."

"I've slept with her for years, but that's not the same thing as her being my mistress."

Silence. Since he couldn't see her from where he stood, he turned. She had not stirred, had made no sign. She responded to his look with a little smile.

"You see!"

"What do I see?"

85

"Nothing . . . I always thought she was the type of woman you liked."

"That depends on what I want her for," he replied crudely.

"Exactly . . . I felt it the very first day. So I always knocked before coming into your office."

"If you want me to, I'll get rid of her."

"Why? In the first place, it isn't her fault. . . . Besides, you would only have to get another. . . ."

It was a curious sensation. François felt as though he'd been set free, but at the same time, there was something abnormal in the atmosphere; it was like walking on boggy ground.

Bébé was so calm! Hadn't it been her idea to marry him? Hadn't she known?

"Does Félix know?" she asked him as she began getting ready for bed.

"He probably suspects. We never talk about such things."

"Ah!"

Why that "ah"?

"And her husband? He doesn't know?"

That made François even more uncomfortable. The husband was an employee of the telephone company. A good man, with a long mustache like old man Donge's. He had had occasion to come to the tannery two or three times to repair the telephone, and he had worked in the office while his wife and François were both there.

"That does it, Monsieur Donge. . . . I think this time it'll stay fixed."

And he held out his big hand, while he discreetly avoided saying good-by to his wife, merely giving her a little glance.

"No; he doesn't know."

"Doesn't it do anything to you to think that at night . . . in that man's bed . . ."

"It's so much less important than you think! . . . If I told you . . ."

"What?"

"Nothing. It's too ridiculous."

"You can say it, because from now on we're friends."

"I've never even called her by her first name. I don't know her. . . . Why, as soon as it's over, without even giving her time to breathe, I begin dictating: . . . *'in reply to yours of'* . . . Did you get that, Madame Flament? You can look up the date on the letter. . . . *I regret to inform you that under the circumstances it will be impossible for us to allow you the reduction you . . .'* "

Bébé laughed. He could not see her face as she bent over the dressing table, but he heard her laugh. Satisfied, he smiled and took off his shoes.

"I see, darling, it's of so little importance! Especially since I'm not your type. . . . Admit it!"

"That depends for what . . . It's certain you never were and never will be good at making love. . . . Anyway, that isn't what counts in life. . . . Are you offended?"

"Why should I be offended? You've been frank."

"You asked me to be, didn't you?"

"Yes."

He wondered at that moment whether he hadn't made a mistake. But she'd wanted this, hadn't she?

"What are you thinking about?" he asked as he got into bed.

They were sleeping in the new twin beds, very modern, that Bébé had ordered. The room had been done over in light colors. There was nothing of the old house about it any longer.

"Nothing . . . About what you said."

"You're not depressed?"

"There's nothing to be depressed about."

"If you mind, it won't happen again. . . . Sometimes days, weeks go by without my touching her. Then, for no reason . . ."

"I understand."

"You can't understand. You're not a man."

She went into their new bathroom. You had to go down a step. In this house you were always going down steps or along rambling hallways.

She stayed for a long time. He began to be worried. He thought she might be crying. He almost went to find out, hesitated, dreading a possible scene.

He had been wise not to, because when she returned, her eyes were dry, her face untroubled.

"Good night, François. Let's go to sleep now."

She kissed him on the forehead, and as soon as she was in bed, turned out the light.


When he glanced up again, the superintendent and Madame Flament were carrying out the filing cabinet and the typewriter. He looked at the two of them as he would have looked at inanimate objects, but met Félix's questioning eyes with somewhat less equanimity.

"What about the contract with the Society of

Great European Hotels?" he asked to cover his embarrassment.

"I signed it last week. I had to give the manager ten thousand francs. . . ."

"Five would have been enough." He let it fall as if feeling he had to revenge himself on someone, even on his brother.

Mechanically, he tore open Olga Jalibert's letter.

*"My dear François:—*
*"I am writing from the Hotel Royal, room 133. Does that remind you of anything? If it weren't for Jacqueline being here . . ."*

Olga Jalibert had a daughter thirteen years old, sharp and secretive, who looked at Donge with hate, as though she understood. And, who knows, perhaps she did understand. Her mother made scarcely any attempt to hide things from her.

*"When I heard of the catastrophe, I knew right away that the best thing for me to do was to get out of the way for a while and, since this is the season for vacations . . . Gaston agreed with me. We didn't say anything, naturally, but I felt that he was worried and was going to try to see you. . . . I have just had a letter from him in which he tells me that you are doing as well as possible and that everything seems to be turning out all right.*

*"I still can't get over Bébé's doing such a thing. But remember what I said when you told me she knew about us! You see, dear, you don't understand a thing*

*about women, especially young girls. And Bébé is
really still a young girl. . . .*

"Well, that's that. I've been so frightened for you
and for everybody. In a little town like ours, you
never know how far scandal will spread.

"Since you're leaving the hospital (according to
what Gaston says in his letter, you'll probably be home
again when this letter arrives—that's why I'm ad-
dressing it to the house) I hope you'll find some way
to run up here. Telephone me before you come, so I
can send Jacqueline to play tennis or something with
her little friends.

"I've loads of things to tell you. I miss you. Better
telephone at mealtimes, without giving your name,
of course, so they won't come shouting it through the
dining room.

"I can't wait to be in your arms. I adore you.

"Your

"Olga."*

"Félix!"

Félix, from where he was sitting, had certainly recognized the handwriting of the letter François still
held in his hand.

"You don't need me this afternoon, do you?"

He saw that Félix misunderstood. For the first time
in his life, perhaps, François sensed disapproval in his
brother's eyes.

Then he smiled, a relaxed smile, one that people
rarely saw, with just a touch of irony for the sake of
appearances.

"I think I'll spend the night at Chestnut Grove. I

still feel the need for rest. . . . Any message for your wife?"

"Nothing special . . . I'll be out Saturday and stay until Monday morning. . . . Wait! I seem to remember she asked me to bring some sweet butter."

"I'll take it."

Suddenly he put his hand over his eyes.

"What is it, François?"

He swayed, as though he were going to faint.

"Nothing . . . Don't worry . . ."

He took his hand away.

"You're still weak."

"Yes . . . A little."

But Félix had noticed a streak of moisture on his brother's cheek.

"See you tomorrow."

"You're leaving without lunch?"

"There'll be something to eat out there."

"You think it's all right for you to drive?"

"Don't worry! . . . About that ten thousand francs . . ."

"I'm sorry; I thought it was the thing to do."

"That's it. I think so too. You were probably right."

Félix did not understand. François himself would have been hard put to explain.

At the same moment, both of them began to listen. They became aware of an unusual sound and couldn't make out where it came from. Finally, they turned toward the door of the adjoining storeroom.

It was Madame Flament, crying in there all alone, with little regular sobs, her arms crossed on her type-writer, her face buried in her arms.

# — 6 —

The sight of a small white convertible in front of
Chestnut Grove was enough to check abruptly his im-
petuous flight. For, ever since he left the city, ever
since he left Quai des Tanneurs, he had been flying,
as to a lover's tryst.

Who could be calling at Chestnut Grove? The gate
was closed. Frowning, he got out to open it, glancing
toward the garden. He recognized, under the orange
umbrella, his sister-in-law, stretched out as usual in a
deck chair. Another woman was sitting in a wicker
chair facing her, but to François, at that distance, she
was only a splash of color.

To reach the garage, he had to pass close to them
along the red gravel drive. As he approached, an enormous black-and-white Great Dane rose from the
ground. Then François knew. It was Mimi Lambert.

92

She suddenly jumped up from her chair and must have said to Jeanne:

"I don't want to see him."

When François came back from putting his car away, leaving the garage doors open, and strolled over to the orange umbrella, he saw his sister-in-law leaning on the gate, Mimi Lambert sitting behind the wheel of the convertible, and, towering above her, the Great Dane on the seat beside her.

Drinks had been served, and François's glance automatically paused on the crystal glasses, which were of an unusual but very delicate design. They were still faintly cloudy from the ice. Twists of lemon peel floated in a pretty red liquid left at the bottom of the glasses.

Jeanne came toward him and, perfectly casual, held out her hand.

"Hello, François. All right now?"

"Hello, Jeanne. And the children?"

"I sent them with Marthe to Four Pines. They'll be home soon."

She went back to her deck chair. Since she did everything with unending energy, the moment she stopped to rest, instinctively, like an animal stretching itself, she chose the horizontal position.

"Mademoiselle Lambert didn't want to meet me, did she?"

"She fled from you, poor thing! Apparently you've been horribly rude to her."

He sat down almost in the same spot he'd been sitting on the Sunday of the great drama, mixed himself a drink, and sipped it slowly while his eyes caressed the house, the garden, the table, the umbrella, in a way that was both deliberate and profound, almost voluptuous. Perhaps weakness had made him more sensitive. A while ago, on the road, he had been in such a hurry to arrive, to catch the first glimpse of the white fence, the red-tiled roof of Chestnut Grove, that his hands kept gripping the wheel.

"I'd have liked to talk to her. . . ."

Tall and ungainly, she was called the Big Mare in town. How old was she now? Thirty-six? Seemingly, she had no age. She had always been the same: too large, solidly built, with almost masculine features and a deep voice. She never wore anything but tailored suits, which accentuated this masculine appearance. At the Old Mill, where she raised Great Danes, she lived in boots and riding breeches.

If strangers, having read of the Old Mill Kennels, asked directions along the road, people would answer with a touch of irony.

"It's the house right in the middle of a bridge. You can't miss it."

Everything about Mimi Lambert was peculiar: her person; this house, eccentrically built on the bridge a little upstream from town; those huge dogs she took out with her in her absurdly small cars; the way her house was furnished . . .

"May I ask what she wanted?"

"Of course. She's like all the rest of them. . . . It's unbelievable how stupid people can be. Here's this Lambert woman, who imagines that she is in some way responsible for what happened. . . ."

Jeanne raised her head a little to look at her brother-in-law, who remained silent.

"Are you listening?"

94

"Excuse me. Yes, I'm listening. . . . I was thinking . . ."

"She said certain things I didn't understand, because I know nothing about what took place. . . . Among other things, that she ought not to have paid any attention to you and should have gone on seeing Bébé. . . . Is it true that you were rude to her?"

It was true. Mimi Lambert had developed a crush on Bébé. Everybody knew about it, and it was even rumored that there was more than friendship between the two women.

François was not jealous. What he objected to was that no matter what hour of the day he entered his wife's room he was sure to find the Big Mare installed there. She barely greeted him. He was made to feel that he was in the way. The conversation would come to a sudden halt. The two women were plainly waiting for him to leave. If he seemed disposed to stay, Mademoiselle Lambert would get up and kiss Bébé on the forehead.

"I'll be going! Until tomorrow, dear . . . I'll bring what I promised you."

Afterward, if François asked:

"What did she promise to bring you?"

Bébé never failed to answer:

"Nothing of any consequence."

This went on for perhaps four years. There was always the smell of the woman's strange cigarettes in Bébé's room.

One day, six months ago now, François had been more annoyed than usual, or at least he had showed it more plainly. He acted as he had so many times in other circumstances. For months, for years, he would

95

put up with all sorts of things from people. Then suddenly, coming to the end of his patience, he would explode.

This time—it was at Chestnut Grove, and, tired after a hard day, he had been looking forward to getting home—he turned to Mademoiselle Lambert, an apparently permanent fixture in Bébé's room, with a cold stare:

"Mademoiselle Lambert, would it be too much to ask you to allow me to see my wife alone once in a while?"

She left without a word—in such a hurry that she forgot her bag. She sent for it the next day, and they did not see her again.

"Shall I go on? Or does it bore you?"

"Please go on."

"I was saying—but you weren't listening—that Mimi Lambert is not really a bad sort. Only I think she's terribly romantic, like all old maids. . . . She came, as she said, to relieve her conscience. Her friendship with Bébé had been more than simply moral support. How did she put it? She had succeeded in giving meaning to Bébé's life. . . . Under the circumstances, she'd had no right, just because of an affront, especially from a man, to desert Bébé. . . . Why are you smiling?"

"I'm not smiling. Go on."

"She wants to see Bébé and comfort her. She talked of asking for a visiting permit. I advised her to let Bébé alone for the moment. . . . They're all outdoing themselves in saying stupid things about her. Yesterday, for example, Madame Lourtie just happened to drop in! You know Lorette Lourtie, the wife of the brewer?"

Vaguely. He knew everybody in town, but people were uninteresting to him. A stout woman with a retreating chin . . .

"We've met at the Milk Foundation. . . . She pretended to want to consult me about the work. As though by chance, she brought along with her the Villard girl, Maître Boniface's niece. I received them here in the garden, and of course I had to give them tea . . . and we were all out of cookies too!

" 'About our poor Bébé . . . ' Then, sighs and headshakings. My opinion is that Boniface sent his niece on purpose to find out what we thought. A sort of conspiracy.

" 'Certain persons—you know how people talk!— say that when she was in Turkey she acquired the drug habit and that, with one of her friends . . .'

"She meant Mimi Lambert! Imagine! Bébé at sixteen—she was just sixteen when we returned to France—already a drug addict! . . .

"But naturally, everybody agreed, *you* would have noticed it and put a stop to it. . . . Let me see, what else did they say? . . . Oh, yes! You know Dominique, the pharmacist, who publishes that weekly review? He goes around telling everyone he's writing an article that's dynamite, that society in this town is going to get what's coming to it. . . . Are you listening?"

François was no longer listening. He was sad. He had just felt a gentle, peaceful breath of the hospital. He remembered his white bed, Sister Adonie with her hands folded over her stomach, the tinkling of her rosary, and, in the shady courtyard, the blue forms of the old men and their halting footsteps. He was hardly out, and yet already homesick for it.

"The children aren't back yet," he remarked, glancing automatically at the hedge.

"It isn't late."

It was noon. If Bébé had been there, the children would have been at the table by now. But, inevitably, with Jeanne there was a certain laxity in the house.

"Where are you going, François?"

"Upstairs a moment."

He had almost said:

"Bébé's room."

It was really that. He felt the need of renewing contact with her other than through the mess of gossip. The moment he entered the dining room's cool twilight smelling of furniture polish and ripening fruit, wasn't it Bébé's order, Bébé's calm he found all over again?

Bébé was the one who had decorated, created the house. These light rooms in pastel shades; these silk curtains letting a subtler sunlight filter through.

The somewhat frail, ethereal character of everything—that was her handiwork.

Between the period of Quai des Tanneurs, when she was modernizing the old Donge house, and what might be called the Mimi Lambert epoch, there had been at least three years. They were the years that held, for him, the fewest memories.

He himself had been operating at full force, in full expansion. The impetus given to his business dated from that period. He had traveled a great deal, alone or with Félix. There had been delicate questions of capital. He went straight ahead, without hesitation, feeling that everything he touched would succeed; and in fact everything did succeed.

Shouldn't Bébé have been satisfied? Whenever he came home, he found her with her mother or her sister. He would kiss her. It was quite all right like this. Hadn't she said she wanted to be her husband's friend? He didn't have time to pay much attention to her, and when he saw her looking depressed, he attributed it to her delicate health.

"I'd like to ask you something, François. . . ."

They had just bought Chestnut Grove, and work on it was beginning.

"Would you mind if we had a child now?"

His first reaction was a frown. He was not expecting such a request, not, at any rate, put forward with such sangfroid, almost like a business proposition.

"You want to have a child?"

"I'd like to. . . ."

"Well, in that case . . ."

On second thought, he was glad; it would give Bébé something to do. She would be less lonely when he was away for several days.

Now he saw her again as she was at that time, pregnant, paler than usual, superintending the work on the house. He thought it his duty to bring her flowers, candy. And when three of the rooms were finished in the autumn, she insisted on spending the winter at Chestnut Grove.

---

99

"Lunch is served."

He gave a start. Marthe had just opened the door and found him sitting on his wife's bed.

"Is Jacques home yet?"

"Everybody's at the table."

He went downstairs. His son did not get up, but looked at him with curiosity, held up his cheek, and, in return, gave an absentminded kiss that just grazed his father's ear. Jeanne's children were there too, napkins tied around their necks.

"What do you say to Uncle François?"

"Hello, Uncle François . . ."

He had to turn his head away to hide his emotion. Then he sat opposite his son. He had just had a curious sensation as he bent over Jacques's face: for an instant he thought he was bending over Bébé. Jacques had the same pallor, the same transparent skin, as well as that detachment, as of a life outside of life.

Why, for years, whenever he spoke of the boy, had he always, without thinking, said, "your son"?

Yet he could not disclaim him, thanks to the Donge nose, that long slanting nose that gave a discordant note to the child's face.

But no one, looking at Jacques, would believe he was looking at a man's son. The boy was a woman's son in every respect, having the same grace, the same weakness and introspectiveness.

Jacques would contemplate his father gravely, as one contemplates a stranger. Sometimes he would come out to the garden or to the garage looking for him, but only when he wanted his fishing line fixed or a toy mended. Never the least effusiveness. Never

100

that warm, confiding, physical intimacy that existed between the boy and his mother.

Was that why François had taken so little interest in him?

By temperament he disliked weak people, or, to be more exact, he ignored them, slighted them without thinking. He had played much more with his sister-in-law's turbulent youngsters than with his own son.

"Eat, Jacques," Jeanne murmured, but not very convincingly. "You know that Mama wouldn't be very pleased if she saw you picking at your food like that."

The boy threw her a black look, watched his father for an instant, then began to eat, but with a sort of contempt.

"Where are you going, François?"

He rose from the table long before the end of the meal and started for the stairs. An impatience that was almost painful had just seized him, was quivering in his chest and making his hands tremble. He had to be alone. It was an obsession; he had to look for Bébé.

How could he possibly not have understood? He strode up and down her room. Like a man whose wife has died, he might almost have opened Bébé's closet to touch the softness of her dresses, to kiss the end of a scarf.

He hadn't understood a thing! Never! It started at Cannes. Or at Royan, the very first day. No, it started long before that, with his childhood, with his mother, whom he had always seen trotting around the house like a worker ant; and who would invariably say, with marked respect:

101

"Mind, now! Here comes your father."

Was there any reason, just because her name was d'Onneville (a counterfeit d', at that) and because she had been brought up in the most fashionable quarter of Constantinople, why she should be treated differently from the wife of the tanner, Donge?

Who had mentioned the word "romantic" a little while ago? Well, life wasn't romantic. It wasn't made up of a young girl's dreams, but of hard realities. Bébé would get used to it like everybody else, and would stop watching it with the eyes of a wild gazelle, as it came toward her.

He was in full possession of his powers, in full ascension. Had he time to worry about a child's moods? And just because she hadn't the least passion, was he supposed to get along without passion for the rest of his life?

Did she finally understand? So much the better! Perhaps she wasn't quite so romantic as she seemed.

He gave her everything she wanted. She didn't like the old people's bedroom on Quai des Tanneurs? All right, my girl. Change it! So long as you don't meddle with my office. . . .

The portraits of Papa and Mama Donge on either side of the bed shocked her? After all, she had never known them. Fine! He would take them down to his own lair.

So long as she didn't try to complicate his existence . . . as she had with Madame Flament! . . . What difference could it make to her, who hadn't the slightest notion of sensual pleasure?

She'd get used to it! She'd get to be like other wives! She'd be all the better for it.

102

As for having anything to do with the business . . . God forbid! A woman who spent two or three hours over her toilet every morning, plastered yolk of egg over her cheeks to keep her complexion, daubed on beauty creams and wrapped her hands in wet towels to keep them white!

"How's everything, dear. All right?"

"All right."

"Did you have a good day?"

"Not bad."

Why couldn't she say she'd had a good day, just to please him? And all those complications:

"Would you mind if we didn't have a baby for two or three years?"

"You're not angry about what I said the other day?"

Then all of a sudden, as though it were a business proposition, to come out with:

"Would you mind if we had a child now?"

Jeanne had had hers the way she ate cakes. And Félix was never met with equivocal glances like those Bébé gave François when he came home.

You'd think sometimes that he was an enemy, or at least an intruder. If she happened to be writing, she would quickly cover it so he couldn't read what she had written.

"What were you doing?"

"Nothing."

"Are you bored?"

"No. And you? Did you have a great deal of work?"

"Yes, a great deal."

"Did you see lots of people?"

"All the people I had to see in a business way."

103

A long thin-lipped smile from her. In moments like these, he wanted to slap her. Or else to leave, saying:

"I'll come back when you can greet me decently."

There had been worse than that. He blushed suddenly when he thought of it. The day she had asked to have a child . . . He was so irritated that he set about it without delay. She did not object. She simply asked him in a natural tone of voice:

"You're sure you are perfectly healthy?"

Because he had mistresses! Because he slept from time to time with Madame Flament! Because, during his trips away from home, he didn't refuse any casual amusement that came his way!

"I am perfectly healthy. You don't need to worry."

And she replied, in that monotone that annoyed him so:

"Then, it's all right."

And out of that, their son had been born.

That day, François felt like saying:

"Well, there's your son for you. Perhaps you'll become a normal woman now. You did want to be Madame Donge . . ."

Now, suddenly, in the almond-green bedroom, he drove his fist at the wall, almost breaking his hand, and muttered in a rage that verged on frenzy:

"Stupid! Stupid! Stupid!"

He! . . . They! . . . Life!

Stupid to keep rubbing each other the wrong way for . . . how long? Ten years! The ten best years of life! . . . Stupid to hurt someone from morning to night . . . Stupid to live side by side, to sleep in the

104

same room, to make a child out of their combined flesh, and to be incapable of understanding each other.

He had come to Chestnut Grove to compose himself, to find Bébé's image, and, faced with that image, which he found everywhere, he was seized with an unbounded indignation against himself.

Why? What aberration had made him fail to understand? Was he a monster, as his wife must have thought? Was he more selfish, blinder than anybody else?

Wasn't he simply a man?

There were days, he realized now, when he had hated her. Many nights he could have come to Chestnut Grove but decided not to at the last moment. It wasn't in order to see a mistress, but to avoid meeting that cold gaze of hers, which judged and condemned. Those nights he would go to bed alone at Quai des Tanneurs, reading until he fell asleep.

"Did you have a great deal of work, yesterday?"

"A great deal."

She didn't believe him. She was convinced that he was having a new affair. And he was sure now that she used to sniff at him when he came home, sniff at his clothes, his breath, trying to catch some foreign odor.

He came from the outside, bringing the air, the vitality of the outside into this house that was as calm and serene as a convent, where Bébé lived bent over a sickly child.

She resents my vitality! he had thought again and again. She's furious about being stuck here in the country because of the child's health. Isn't this the fate of many women? My mother, did she . . . ? Or is it because Bébé is a d'Onneville?

Never a word of reproach. She was too proud to reproach him. On the contrary, the more she detested him, the more suspicions and grievances she nurtured against him, the more carefully she watched every detail of her behavior toward him. Probably wanting it said of her in town:

"Bébé Donge is an ideal wife and mother."

If he came home in his car, she would go out to the garage to meet him, holding Jacques by the hand.

"Say hello to Daddy."

She would smile, a joyless smile.

"Did you have a great deal of work?"

"A great deal."

He began to read a double meaning into everything she said. "Did you have a great deal of work" really meant:

"You were having a good time, weren't you? While I, alone here . . ."

Was it his fault she had a delicate constitution and their child was growing up long and pale, like an asparagus? Should he give up living, give up taking on new projects, building, leading the life he knew he was meant for?

He saw things clearly. Even when he was small, people said:

"He has terrible little eyes. They see right to the bottom of things."

So she was jealous, jealous of everything: of women, his office, his business, the cafés he frequented, the automobiles he drove; jealous of his free-

106

dom to go and come as he pleased, of the air he breathed, of his health, of . . .

One day, when he was driving back to town, exasperated, talking half aloud to himself, he suddenly hit upon another idea: Bébé had married him because she was jealous of her sister, jealous of that couple they formed, her sister and Félix, at Royan, walking in front of them with the heedless air of those who are already living in the future.

Why shouldn't she have a husband, be part of a couple too? Was she going to stay alone with her mother? How much longer would she be dragged from one watering place to another, from one dance to another?

Very well! She'd do the same as Jeanne. And so she arranged her life to suit herself. She played in her room with her lotions and creams like a little girl with her dolls; she played with her son; she played with her house, which she kept changing all the time. . . .

She was always correct in her behavior toward her husband, but she never talked to him about herself, or about themselves.

He decided he would act in just the same way. Thereafter he arrived at Chestnut Grove, changed his clothes, strolled around the garden, prepared the tennis court, waited for Félix to arrive for a game. . . . Wasn't she jealous of Félix too? Weren't they, he and Félix, the Donge family as opposed to the d'Onnevilles?

There was one person who understood him, Olga Jalibert. She wasn't even intelligent, but she had intuition.

"It's your misfortune to have a wife who isn't a

woman but a young girl . . . and, what's more, she'll always be that. She's incapable of keeping up with you. Her dream is to float down a river all her life in a poetic scene murmuring sentimental twaddle to the man rowing opposite her."

But Olga had a sense of reality. She understood love. Above all, she understood men.

"If you keep on the way you've been going, you'll soon be the most powerful man in this city. Then, if you want to, you will go even farther. . . . Just remember what I'm telling you."

She said these words as she sat naked on the bed, smoking and fondling her little brown breasts, which he'd just been biting.

"We should have met sooner. . . . Gaston can't do a thing unless there's somebody there to push him. You and I together . . ."

Had Bébé recognized Olga's odor? It was very possible. Very possible too that she had sniffed at his skin after he'd gone to sleep.

"I'd like to give you a piece of advice, François. Don't think I'm jealous. But you should be careful about Madame Jalibert. I may be mistaken, but I have the impression she wants to push you too far."

Well, well! Did she, in addition, have a business sense, and was she afraid for their fortune? Only the day before, Olga had indeed spoken to him about plans for a hospital, a hospital in which he would be one of the chief stockholders. . . .

"Don't worry. I know what I'm doing."

He had put money into the hospital—almost in defiance.

What could anyone object to? He gave his wife

all the money she wanted. His businesses prospered. He stayed at Chestnut Grove as often as he could. He had simple tastes. He spent hardly anything on himself. There had never been the least scandal connected with any of his love affairs.

She could ask anyone in town she pleased. Anyone would tell her:

"The Donge brothers know what they want. They'll go far. . . ."

In spite of a young chit with too much imagination, who had dresses that cost thousands of francs sent down from Paris, to be worn on solitary walks in a remote country garden, and who amused herself translating English poetry with Mimi Lambert.

That is what they did, the two of them. With the ardor as if the world depended on it! When François came to the country to relax for a few hours in the fresh air, Clo, the cook, would bustle up to him with:

"You forgot the mushrooms!"

Or the sweet butter, or something else they couldn't obtain in Ornaie.

"Will you take a look at the faucet in the laundry?"

And in his pajamas he would go to fix the faucet, or to roll the tennis court. During that time, the curtains of the bedroom remained drawn until ten or eleven o'clock. At last, dressed as though for a garden party, with the lingerie of an experienced coquette, Bébé would come downstairs, lithe and graceful, a fixed smile on her lips.

"Aren't you dressed yet, François? Lunch will be ready in a moment."

———

"What are you doing?"

He stopped, saw that he was standing in the middle of the room but forgot that he had just been pacing furiously.

"What's the matter, François?"

Jeanne was there, looking a little frightened. Glancing at himself in the three-panel mirror, he saw a haggard face with feverish eyes and hair disarranged. He had torn open his tie, and it dangled on either side of his neck.

"I wonder if it was wise for you to come here to rest. . . . Perhaps it would have been better for you to be home with Félix. . . . You think too much."

He looked at her with a bitter smile, seeing her upset and, as always, anxious to restore peace and calm around her.

"Perhaps if you took a little trip somewhere . . . We've never understood Bébé—any of us. I think she's like our father, who . . . Some other time I'll tell you about that. . . . Mother would be furious."

"Jeanne! Tell me something!"

She was startled by his brusqueness.

"Answer me frankly. Do you think I'm a normal husband, a good husband?"

"But . . ."

"Answer!"

"Of course."

"You're convinced I'm a good husband?"

"Aside from a few peccadillos, which are common gossip . . . But that's of so little importance! I'm sure that Félix . . . So long as I don't know it, that it doesn't happen under our roof . . ."

"You're wrong! I tell you, Jeanne, I'm a monster.

110

I'm an imbecile. . . . An idiot, a poor idiot! You hear me? . . . I—I'm the one responsible for this!"

"Calm yourself, François, please! The children are downstairs eating. . . . Jacques has been nervous these last few days. Yesterday he asked me again . . ."

"Well?"

"He asked me . . . You frighten me, François. . . . Well, if you must know, he asked me what crime his mother had committed. . . . I didn't know what to answer."

"You want to know what to answer? Tell him that his mother committed the crime of loving his father too much!"

"François!"

"Don't be afraid. I haven't gone crazy. I know what I'm saying. . . . Please go now! Give me a few more minutes. . . . In a little while I'll come down and be calm. . . . And don't say anything to Jacques. One day, I'll talk to him myself. . . . If you only knew, my poor Jeanne, how stupid men can be!"

And he repeated, holding back his clenched fist, which he felt like driving into the wall again:

"Stupid! Stupid! Stupid!"

"You really want me to . . . It isn't very interesting, you know. They tried to be happy, like you, like us. . . . They did the best they could. Now, Father is dead. . . . And at this moment . . ."

Through the open window came the cool night breeze. The moon was just rising above the dark mass of trees. The children were in bed. The maids were finishing the dishes in the kitchen.

All one could see of Jeanne, deep in her armchair, was a pale form and the lighted end of her cigarette, its odor mingling with the heady scent of the night.

". . . at this moment, Mother, wearing her big white coat, is leaving the Pension Berthollat, walking along the Promenade des Anglais, past the crowded benches, toward the Casino Municipal. . . . If her rheumatism has started up again, as it always does in the Midi, she is walking with a cane. It gives her—I don't know why—the air of a great lady in exile. . . . Sometimes, when she isn't playing baccarat, Mother really looks like a queen."

François sat very still, not smoking, not making the slightest sound. Because he had on a dark suit, his presence was discernible only by the milky blur of his face in the dark.

"I think we'd better have the window closed . . . weak as you are."

"I'm not cold."

He was, in fact, wrapped in a steamer rug like an invalid. Upstairs, a little while ago, in Jeanne's presence, he had fainted. True, it had lasted only a moment. Jeanne had hardly picked up the receiver to call Dr. Pinaud when he regained consciousness.

"It isn't necessary."

At the hospital, Levert had given him pills to take in case of such an event; all he had to do was to take one of them. Now, he was in the passive state of a convalescent. He had wanted this dark room, this bay window open on the night, looking out toward the trees, this odor of humus, and the monotonous song of the crickets.

"If you knew Stambul, you would understand more easily. The whole foreign colony lived up on the hill, in the suburb of Pera, which is an entirely modern city. . . . We had a large apartment in a seven-story building, all white and brand-new, and our windows looked over the roofs of the native city and the Golden Horn. . . . Didn't Bébé ever show you the photographs?"

Perhaps, long ago, but he had paid no attention.

113

Jeanne's words left him thoughtful. Hadn't Bébé, at the very beginning of their marriage, said:

"I wish I had known your father. . . ."

And here, after ten years, he was feeling the same sort of curiosity!

"I don't think life in Turkey now is what it was then. When we were there, it was very gay. Mother was beautiful. She was considered the most beautiful woman in Pera. Father was tall and thin; he had an aristocratic air, or at least that's what I've always heard people say."

"How did he get started?"

"He went there as an engineer. . . . If poor Mother knew I was telling you all this! Oh, well! . . . You're sure you don't want me to close the window? Or have Clo make you a hot drink? . . . Father's career moved rapidly. It is said, and I think it's true, that it was really Mother who made him. . . . The French ambassador at that time was a bachelor. We were always going to the embassy, where there were luncheons and dinners all the time. The ambassador kept asking Mother's advice about this and that. In the end, she became, unofficially, the hostess of the embassy. . . . You understand?"

"And your father?"

"I remember an amusing detail. As soon as he was appointed director of docks, Mother made him wear a monocle, and it gave Father a nervous tic. . . . You asked if he knew the truth? . . . I'm not sure. I was too young, and I was mostly with the servants. We had three or four. Our house was a veritable mad-house: Mother dressing, ordering everybody around, running through the apartment; the telephone always ringing, callers constantly arriving; and her earrings couldn't be found anywhere, or her dress hadn't been delivered in time. . . .

" 'When did Monsieur go out? . . . Get me his office . . .'

" 'Hello! Hello! Is Monsieur d'Onneville there? This is Madame d'Onneville. . . . He hasn't come yet? . . . Thank you.'

"Mother was jealous, insanely jealous. With the aid of the telephone, she tracked Father all around town.

" 'Hello! You haven't seen Monsieur d'Onneville yet? . . . He's just left? . . . No, nothing, thank you.'

"And my poor father never said a thing. He was like a big greyhound, elegant and docile. Whenever he was disconcerted, he would begin endlessly polishing his monocle, while his eyelid twitched.

" 'If you go out, take at least one of your daughters with you!'

"He began by taking me. When I went to boarding school, Bébé took my place as chaperone."

"Hand me a cigarette, will you please?"

"You don't think it's bad for you?"

"Of course not!"

He felt relaxed. His very weakness gave him a sense of well-being. He took deep breaths of the night without knowing if it was the night of Chestnut Grove, or of the Baie des Anges, or of the Bosporus.

"Go on."

"What do you want me to tell you? . . . Father used to take one or the other of us with him, sometimes both, since he was forced to. Soon we would notice that he was embarrassed.

115

" 'I have a little matter to attend to, girls. I'll leave you at this tearoom for a little while, and you can have a pastry while you're waiting. . . . But you mustn't tell your mother.'

"It was sometimes difficult, because when we got home, Mother always questioned us. We had to tell her everything in detail, the streets we had taken, the people we had met . . .

" 'How could you possibly have spent three thousand francs again, in three days?'

" 'I assure you . . .'

"This while they were dressing to go to some dinner party. There was one almost every night in one of the embassies or legations, at a banker's or some rich Levantine's. . . . Bébé and I stayed home with the servants.

"Toward the end, Mother grew even worse, but I wasn't there any longer. I was at the Ursuline Convent at Therapia. It was Bébé . . .

"Father must have cheated all his life, from morning to night, concealed things, schemed, piled up lies big and small, secured accomplices, including the servants.

" 'Don't tell Madame that . . .'

"Then he died. Everyone thought Mother would become Madame Ambassador, but she didn't, and we returned to France. . . . You see why poor Mother's like a lost soul here? . . . She was the beautiful Madame d'Onneville. She reigned. She gave orders. And then suddenly she was nothing but a stout middle-aged woman in a provincial city. . . . I wanted to buy her a dog for company. Do you know what she said?

" 'Oh, naturally! You too! So I'll really look like an

old woman! No thank you, daughter!. When I've reached that point, I think I'd rather die.' "

They could hear Jacques tossing in his bed overhead. He seldom had a peaceful sleep.

"Well, we're all born into some family or other," Jeanne concluded, with an attempt at indifference. "Each family has its own way of living. In ours, everyone went his own way. We met by chance. Like billiard balls that hit each other by chance, and then shoot off in another direction. When disorder is the order of the day, of every day, you don't notice it, and it doesn't bother you. . . ."

François's eyes were turned toward her. He could see nothing but the white splash of her dress. Yet it seemed to him that he was seeing his sister-in-law for the first time. He had never bothered about her. Did he ever pay attention to anything that didn't touch him personally? He had always looked upon her as an amiable, energetic girl who smoked cigarettes and rattled along about everything, without thinking, in a rather shrill voice.

"Was Bébé as secretive as her father, then?" he asked after a moment of hesitation.

"The truth is, I've never really known her. She was too young for me. She used to steal my powder, perfumes, and creams. From the time she was a child, she had a passion for clothes. When you didn't see her around anywhere, you could be sure she was in her room, in front of the mirror, trying on the dresses and hats she'd stolen from Mother or me. She'd twist them around in her own way. . . . Except for that, I don't think I ever saw her play. She never had dolls. She never had little playmates, as I did. . . .

117

"She knew only the worst period, when the scenes between Mother and Father occurred with depressing regularity. . . . She was always being left alone with the servants."

"What's the matter?" François interrupted. He had noticed a hesitation in his sister-in-law's voice.

"Oh, well, what's the difference, now that I'm telling you. . . . What I wonder is how she kept it to herself for so long. I even wonder if . . . At any rate, one day—it was four or five years ago, not more, since Jacques was walking already—she came to see me with him while I happened to be sorting out old photographs. Naturally, I showed them to her, one by one.

" 'You remember So-and-So? . . . I thought he was taller than that. . . .'

"Then I came across a snapshot of her when she must have been thirteen. In the same picture you could see one of our maids, a Greek girl whose name I've forgotten.

" 'Funny to think you used to look like that,' I said.

"I saw her blush. Then she grabbed the photograph out of my hand and nervously tore it up.

" 'What's got into you?'

" 'I don't want to remember that girl.'

" 'Wasn't she nice to you?'

" 'If you only knew . . .'

"I can still see Bébé pacing up and down and that bitter expression on her face.

" 'I'll tell you. . . . Today I'm able to talk about it.'

"Poor Bébé, she began to tremble at the mere recollection. . . .

"Have you a cigarette? . . . You really don't want me to close the window? The mist's beginning to rise."

A white vapor was floating up from the dewy grass, forming a fine veil a few feet above the ground, with long shreds and tatters.

"I don't know what I would have done in her place, but I hardly think I'd have kept it to myself. . . . Of course, she was only twelve. It was one of the many times she'd been left alone in the house with a maid—the Greek girl in the snapshot. Bébé may have been playing a game, or it was for some other reason she had hidden in the laundry room. A little later the Greek girl came in with her lover—a policeman, as far as I can remember. . . . You can imagine Bébé's feelings. She didn't dare call out, she didn't dare stir. . . . Once, the man said:

" 'I think I hear someone.'

"And the maid replied:

" 'If it's the kid, it's just too bad for her. . . . But after what she's seen, you don't need to mind in front of her.'

"Bébé was sick from it for several days. But she didn't say a word to Mother or to anybody."

Why did François just then recall the moment when, in their hotel room at Cannes, he had gone over to the window and lighted a cigarette?

"I can't think of anything else. . . ." Jeanne sighed. "It's time for you to go to bed."

"Not yet."

François's voice was affectionate. Never before had he felt so close to his sister-in-law. It seemed to him that he had just discovered her, and that from now on he had a friend.

"Has she ever talked to you about me?"

"In what way?"

"I don't know. . . . She might have complained. She might have . . ."

"Did you quarrel sometimes?"

"Never."

It was Jeanne's turn to be thoughtful.

"It's funny—the difference between brothers. . . . Of course, you could say the same about sisters. You seem to be a happy couple, you and Bébé, like two sensible people who don't want to complicate existence. After all, what's the use? . . . Take Félix and me. He comes, he goes; I come, I go. We are together and we are happy. He leaves, and we are still happy. What would happen if we began trying to . . ."

"To what?" he asked softly when she left the sentence hanging.

"Hell! How do I know?"

She stood up. It was as though she were shaking off the humidity of the night that was seeping through both of them like a mysterious distress.

"What's the use of asking oneself questions all the time? We do the best we can, as our parents did the best they could, and as our children will do the best they can. . . . Come along! I think I'd better get you to bed now."

"Bébé has been very unhappy," François said without stirring.

"That's her concern! We all make our own happiness, or unhappiness."

"Or others make it for us."

"What do you mean? You think you've made her unhappy? Because of Olga? Do you think it was because Bébé found out about you that she did what she did?"

"No."

"Well, then? Do I ask Félix what he's been up to when he comes home from a business trip? I don't want to know! I once told him that so long as I don't see it and it doesn't happen in our own house, so long as . . ."

"You don't mean it."

"I do mean it!"

She almost shouted this, stamping her foot on the floor.

"You know very well you don't."

"So? What good would it do . . . ? Tell me, François, have you been that way all your married life, you and Bébé? . . . You spend hours questioning yourselves and asking yourselves if . . . and if . . ."

"No. That's just it!"

"Why 'that's just it'?"

"Bébé has always been alone."

"Isn't everybody alone? . . . Come along now. Get up. Else you'll be fainting again . . ."

She closed the window with finality and snapped on the switch. In the sudden flood of light, they avoided looking at each other.

"Shouldn't you take a sleeping pill? Are you sure a hot drink wouldn't help? . . . As you like. You hear—the maids are going up to bed."

She bustled around, trying to be her usual cheerful self again.

"Up with you, François! Tomorrow . . ."

Tomorrow, what?

Why had he bristled when Bébé, barely arrived at the house on Quai des Tanneurs, looking at the

121

portrait of old man Donge, and his walrus mustache, had said humbly, or timidly:

"I wish I had known your father . . ."?

It wasn't an idle remark. Unlike her sister, Bébé never made senseless remarks. She wasn't merely being polite either.

Bébé felt conscious of having come from far away, of bringing with her, in her, something of her father, who had had to rely on his servants' complicity; of her mother and her mother's magnificent myopia; and of a Pera teeming with festivities and languors.

For eighteen years, her little brain had been at work all alone, and also all alone she had tried to efface the ugly memory of the Greek girl and the policeman sordidly making love on the table in the laundry room.

Then, at Royan, she had put him at ease. She had immediately understood the role of the little dancer, Betty or Daisy. She had told him so. . . .

It wasn't marriage she wanted, as he had so egotistically imagined. She had had an example of marriage before her eyes. And it certainly wasn't sexual intercourse, the mere thought of which made her turn pale.

She had entered the house on Quai des Tanneurs frozen with apprehension. She had entered with the man who was to be her companion forever. She had looked at the walls, tried to feel the quality of the atmosphere, took in all the familiar odors, and, in front of the portraits, murmured:

"I wish I had known your father. . . ."

Because perhaps then it would have been easier for them to understand each other.

She had gone to his office, had looked tenderly at

the place where François sat, the part of the quay that, framed by the window, was in front of his eyes all day long.

"Don't you think I could . . ."

And he hadn't understood! Wasn't a wife's place upstairs in the apartment? Let her arrange the house to suit herself! Let her do her job as a wife: see the tradesmen, the painters, the decorators, give the cook orders for meals, and try to make useful connections in the city.

He had advised her to do this.

"After you've made a few friends, as you soon will, you won't be bored."

"I'm not bored."

Maternally, Jeanne lighted his bed lamp, looked to see that there was water in his carafe, that the bed was turned down.

"Promise me you'll go to bed right away? Can I leave you without worrying?"

He wanted to hug her. For ten years he had looked upon her as a great good-natured girl of no interest. So that was why she busied herself with all those charities, where she had the reputation of being a bungler.

"Don't think too much, François; it's much better not to! . . . Good night, François."

She went into Jacques's room to make sure he was asleep, that he wasn't uncovered, then into her own children's room, and finally he heard her getting undressed in her own room, heard her sink heavily into bed, where, before going to sleep, she would smoke a final cigarette.

Should he go back as far as Madame Flament?

At the thought of Madame Flament, sweat came out on his forehead. It seemed impossible, monstrous. If that's the way it was, there was no hope. To think that because at a certain moment his body felt a physical need of no consequence, which dictated his actions . . .

Back to Cannes, where he was awkwardly rowing the little boat, embarrassed by the amused glances of the sailors on the yachts . . .

It was so human! The fatigue after a night in the train, after all the wedding ceremonies, the traditional banquet . . . his legitimate desire to take possession of his wife . . . The way she insisted on going out in that rowboat . . .

He couldn't sleep. He tossed and turned in his bed and thought to himself that Jeanne must be listening to every sound, afraid of another fainting spell. But it was out of rage that he had fainted in the afternoon, rage because . . .

He was no longer emotional. He was trying to understand, objectively, almost scientifically. He hated vagueness, halfway solutions. He had always been a practical man.

He was not thinking of Bébé. Bébé was no longer the problem. It was he himself.

Why, through what aberration, had he lived with her so long without understanding her? How could he have misunderstood her to the point of hating her?

"I wish I had known your father. . . ."

Didn't that show that she, on her side, had made an effort?

And that night, when she had sat beside a sleeping François, who was breathing with difficulty on his left side . . .

He was her man. Her companion. And he was sleeping there next to her skin, next to her flesh. His eyes closed, he was perhaps dreaming, and she knew nothing of his dreams. Even when his eyes were open, could she penetrate his thoughts?

"I was thinking . . . that from now on we are always going to live together. . . ."

She had seen two people, her father and mother, living together. Had been their witness, almost their accomplice.

"Promise me, no matter what happens, that you will always be frank with me . . ."

He turned over in his sticky sheets.

"What's the use," Jeanne had said, sighing philosophically in the shadowy darkness, "of asking oneself questions all the time? We do the best we can. . . . Do I ask Félix when he comes home from a business trip . . ."

Was Jeanne right, after all? Was she unhappy? Was Félix unhappy? Weren't their children growing as naturally as plants?

Wasn't it Bébé who was wrong to aspire to the impossible, wrong to . . . ?

Without thinking, he stretched out his arm, and he would have given anything at that moment to feel his wife's thin body beside him, that body which had so deeply disappointed him by its flabbiness. It seemed to him that if she had been there, if he had been able to hold her tightly in his arms, they would have known, both of them, an embrace such as one knows only in dreams, a soaring of souls freed from all materiality.

He was sweating. Since his accident, he sweated profusely, and his sweat had a strong odor. On Quai des Tanneurs too, strong odors were always present: among others, the smell of tannin, which had been familiar to him ever since he could remember. Returning home from a business trip, he would sniff it with delight, the way one welcomes in the country the smell of manure and burning logs.

Perhaps it would have been enough to take her by the hand? . . . Did Félix take Jeanne by the hand? Had his father taken his mother by the hand? Had they been unhappy? . . . Can a man do a man's job, set up factories, a cheese-making plant, a hog farm, and at the same time . . .

No! He could think of good arguments but he was wrong just the same. A man didn't have the right to take a person, a heedless young girl at the seashore, at Royan, bring her to his house, and then abandon her to her solitude.

Not even to *her* solitude—to solitude in a strange atmosphere, one that might well seem hostile!

How could he have believed that the fact of being his wife would be enough for Bébé?

Still another recollection, another piece of evidence that had escaped him, but now threw light, not on Bébé but on himself: She was in the hospital, expecting the baby at any moment. He had thought it his duty to stay with her, at least during the first hours of her confinement. He held her hand. The chair was uncomfortable. He was unable to keep his mind from

126

wandering to business matters. Between two pains she asked him, almost imploringly:

"You do love me a little, don't you, François?"

And he answered without hesitation, sure that it was true:

"If I hadn't loved you, I wouldn't have married you."

She turned her head away, and the next instant her face was distorted by another pain.

When she opened her eyes a few hours later, still bleary from the anesthetic, and they showed her her baby, hadn't her first words been:

"Does he look like you?"

It had brought tears to his eyes, and when he left the hospital ten minutes later, there was still a lump in his throat. Then, taking the key out of his pocket, he started his car and plunged into the sunshine flooding the street.

A hundred yards farther and it was over, forgotten. He was once more François Donge. Once more his feet were firmly planted in what he considered reality.

How long had she struggled in her void?

Thinking of her now, he was reminded of a fly he had seen one evening at Chestnut Grove which had fallen into the brook. At first the fly did not believe in the inevitable. It moved its legs frantically, fluttered its wings, as though an effort might still restore it to the life-giving air. Its movements made it turn in a circle. There was an oak leaf that formed a floating island, on which François thought it would succeed in getting a foothold.

A few moments of immobility. Fatigue, perhaps?

Caution? Not to use up all its strength? Then, once more a desperate struggle, a prodigious effort, circles growing wider and wider on the moiréd surface of the water.

But the wings were wet by this time. The eddies were growing in depth rather than diameter. For the fly, what a yawning chasm that dark icy water, which was only a black hole, must have seemed.

François was leaning against the trunk of a willow tree, smoking a cigarette.

If a fish . . .

Had the fly any idea that the oak leaf was salvation? It kept on moving its little legs, but, soaked as they were now, they had less purchase on the water. François might have cut a switch and pushed the leaf toward the fly.

He preferred to watch to the end. . . . But he hadn't seen the outcome after all. Exhausted, the fly, after minutes of immobility, was moving again. . . .

"François! François!" cried Jeanne, who was at Chestnut Grove that day, "Come! We're going to eat!"

Hadn't Bébé tried a hundred, a thousand times . . . What he had taken for indifference, or for reserve . . .

She had accepted Madame Flament. . . . Every night, he felt sure, when he was kissing her mechanically on the forehead or cheek, she must have smelled him, wondering if that very day . . .

And he was high-spirited, full of energy. He had worked well. His affairs were looking up. The will of the Donges was creating something new in the city. A hundred, two hundred, five hundred people were

128

dependent now on the Donges, on Donge enterprises, the efforts of François and his brother.

"As of this morning we're the official contractors for the Quartermaster Corps."

"Ah!"

She smiled politely, and he resented her not sharing his enthusiasm. But then, hadn't she spent the whole day in the cold of her solitude?

"Doesn't that please you?"

"But of course . . . Are you going out this evening?"

"I have to see the lawyer about a contract."

"I wanted to show you the curtains I've chosen for the little reception room."

A vague gesture. That was her affair, and hers alone. If he had to bother his head about curtains for the reception room too . . . Weren't the ones that were there before, the ones that dated from his parents' day, good enough for him?

"I'll be late. So don't wait up for me."

Always, he brought back with him, in every wrinkle of his clothes, in the pores of his skin, the stimulating air of the outside world.

"Are you asleep?"

She did not reply. He knew that she was not asleep. It irritated him, and yet, if she pretended to be asleep, it was so he wouldn't know she'd stayed awake waiting for him, listening for the slightest sound.

He hadn't understood a thing!

"If I hadn't loved you, I wouldn't have married you."

Therefore, since he had married her . . .

A thin line of light was growing wider. A bulging silhouette, hair done up in curlers.

"Listen, François," Jeanne scolded, "you'd better take something to make you sleep. You've been turning and tossing and sighing in your bed for an hour. I'll give you twenty drops. . . . Here, drink it! . . . If this goes on, the whole house will have nerves as bad as my sister's!"

# – 8 –

"Sit down, Monsieur Donge . . ."

Then, following his courtroom tactics, Maître Boniface allowed a long pause to intervene, during which he took a pinch of snuff, carelessly stuffing it up his nostrils and staring at François as fiercely as an examiner looks at a candidate.

"I believe we have met before, at my sister-in-law's—Desprez-Mouligne?"

"That was my brother, Félix."

Not being able to smoke in court, Maître Boniface must have acquired the habit of taking snuff. He did it untidily. Grains were scattered through his gray beard and down his dickey. His robe was the shiniest in the courthouse. His nails were dirty. He carried his filthiness in an almost aggressive manner, as the exterior sign of his integrity.

François had been met at the door by the most

disagreeable and ugliest clerk in town. The wide hall was painted to resemble marble and had taken on the color of an old billiard ball. The house reeked—a smell of dishwater.

Boniface was a widower. His only daughter was hunchbacked. And no doubt for fear that his office would seem too gay, although it was already somber enough with its dark furniture, he had had stained glass put in the lower sash of the windows.

"It goes without saying that if you had filed a complaint, or if you had been summoned as a witness by the state, I would not have asked you to come to see me."

François felt as intimidated, as lost as he had been on his first day at school, which was the first time he had come in contact with the world outside his family, and the attorney's office was as gloomy as an antechamber in the courthouse. In it one felt like so much judicial dough that Maître Boniface would soon begin to knead with steady and ferocious energy.

The carpet was worn; the room, overly furnished, smelled of very old paper.

Deliberately and with the same flourish with which he took snuff, Maître Boniface unfolded an enormous handkerchief, buried his nose in it, and blew stentoriously four or five times. Then he inspected the result with interest and carefully folded the handkerchief again.

There was something else that made François feel ill at ease: he had never called upon Maître Boniface, either in an advisory capacity or to be represented in any of the civil suits in which his business often involved him. Instead, he had al-

132

ways consulted a young lawyer whom Boniface despised. He felt like apologizing. It was inexcusable. Maître Boniface was the only lawyer in town—that is, the only one worthy of the name; he was the lawyer of all the families that were of the least importance, and whose secrets he knew better than any confessor.

"Your mother-in-law is a Chartier, I believe? . . . Curiously, I knew her slightly when I was young. . . . She had a brother, Fernand, who was a cavalry lieutenant at Saumur at the same time as a cousin of mine. This cousin inherited a little place a few kilometers from the Chartiers' house. Old man Chartier was departmental treasurer. . . . I remember he suffered from gout. . . . As for Fernand Chartier, he was involved in a rather nasty affair over cards at Monte Carlo and died young in the colonies. . . . Did you know about that?"

"Vaguely."

On the desk in front of Boniface, under his big, hairy, and somewhat grimy hand, a salmon-colored folder bore, in round letters, the words "Donge Case." It was there, inside, that Bébé Donge . . .

"And the d'Onneville your mother-in-law married . . . If I'm not mistaken, he was from the North, from Lille or Roubaix. An engineer who, directly after his marriage, accepted a position in Turkey. . . Eugénie Chartier at that time was one of the most beautiful women in the whole district. . . ."

His hand kept opening and closing the dossier. François was wondering when Boniface would finally get around to his subject, when suddenly, without preamble, he attacked it:

133

"You see, Monsieur Donge, the most regrettable thing about our case is the weapon chosen by my client. Juries sometimes forgive a pistol shot or a blow with a knife, although provincial juries are more severe than juries in Paris. *They never show any indulgence toward women poisoners!* In a way, they are not wrong. It is almost impossible to plead a crime of passion if poison is used. Under the sway of a violent emotion, a person might fire a revolver or seize a hatchet and strike a sudden blow. It is difficult to admit that such an emotion would last long enough and at such a pitch to allow anyone to procure the poison, wait for a favorable moment, and perform all the necessary little actions. . . ."

Another pinch of snuff, without taking his eyes off François, who had rarely felt so uncomfortable in his life. This was undoubtedly the first time that he'd been so completely at a loss. He failed to recognize the drama, or himself, or Bébé, in this Donge case as it came out of the dossier under the lawyer's heavy paw.

"My client, moreover, has been imprudent enough to admit that she procured the poison three months before the crime. Do you know our chief public prosecutor? I can foresee the effects he will wring out of such a statement. May I ask you, Monsieur Donge, the provisions of your marriage contract?"

"We didn't sign a marriage contract."

He answered obediently, in an expressionless voice, like a schoolboy. He felt depressed. In this office with its black furniture, its faded ornaments, its colored windowpanes that dimmed the light, he

134

would have been unable to summon even his wife's silhouette, her face, her hair!

"Community property, then . . . That hardly facilitates my task. . . . What is your estimate of the value of your estate?"

"It's difficult to say."

"Roughly?"

"In a forced sale, the tannery would not be worth very much. . . . But the cheese-making plant, the land, the buildings, the material, cost more than twelve hundred thousand francs. As for . . ."

"What income do you derive from it . . . from everything together?"

"About six hundred thousand francs, for my brother and myself."

"That's right; you and your brother are partners. Let's estimate your share of the capital as somewhat more than two million. The public prosecutor will say three."

"I don't see the connection," François ventured timidly.

"You mean the connection between these figures and my client's act. That is because, Monsieur Donge, you are ignorant of the fact that poisonings nine times out of ten, ninety-five times out of a hundred, are perpetrated for financial gain. In the other five cases it is usually a woman who wishes to get rid of her husband in order to marry her lover. That's what we find so often on farms: a peasant woman who wants to marry her farmhand and resorts to rat poison to make herself a widow."

The handkerchief was unfolded again; the trumpet blew. Maître Boniface heaved a sigh of satisfaction and fell silent, gazing at his visitor.

"I hasten to add that I do not believe that to be the case here. Nevertheless, not knowing on what grounds the state will base its case, we must foresee everything and be prepared. I could cite an instance, the Martineau case, in which one of my illustrious Parisian colleagues had prepared his brief with the most minute attention to detail. Well, the public prosecutor at the trial presented the question in such a way . . . ."

François was perspiring. Had he been asked suddenly where he was, he would have found it difficult to answer. He felt that he was nowhere—nowhere in either time or space. This was like the torture of waiting rooms, even worse. And the voice of the dirty, bearded lawyer went on, complacent, emphatic, pitiless:

"Two million, that's quite a sum, Monsieur Donge! I can't tell what sort of a jury we will have. They're chosen by lot. Among them will be little shopkeepers worried about bills of a few hundred francs, clerks, and men living on a modest income. When they hear the sum of two million . . . And there is another detail that perhaps hasn't occurred to you: What proof have we that Sunday, the twentieth of August, was the first time you took arsenic in your coffee?"

"But . . . ."

"Let me finish!"

He was like an ogre who must eat, with teeth, beard, his whole bulk, set in motion by his inordinate appetite.

"My client has admitted that she took the arsenic

136

from your laboratory three months before. Now everyone knows, if only from reading newspaper accounts of actual crimes or the reports of court proceedings, that death from arsenic poisoning may appear natural if administered progressively and, at the beginning, in infinitesimal doses. What is there to prove that you have not been absorbing just such infinitesimal doses without being aware of it?"

François opened his mouth, but was not given a chance to speak. A peremptory gesture, by a hand with dirty fingernails, cut him short.

"Let us consider the facts coldly, as is proper. We shall forget the motives for the moment. What we know is that these motives, whatever they were, existed three months ago, since my client at that time, running the risk of being caught, took a bottle of arsenic from your laboratory. During those three months you have been going regularly to Chestnut Grove."

That name, on the lips of Maître Boniface! Impossible to connect it with the house he knew, so bright, so orderly.

". . . You slept there, you ate there, you drank coffee there. Many times you have, all of you, your mother-in-law, your brother, your sister-in-law, been together in the garden where the event occurred. . . . For three months, then, the same conditions, which we shall call favorable, existed. The same motives. Why, then, should my client have waited so long? . . . Let me finish, Monsieur Donge! My duty is to consider every possible hypothesis, and you must believe me when I repeat that Monsieur Roy, the public prosecutor, will not fail to do so. . . .

137

"Did your wife bring you a dowry when you were married?"

Had François suddenly found himself indecently dressed, wearing only shorts, for example, in Maître Boniface's office, he could not have been more uncomfortable.

"No. I refused to . . ."

"Did your sister-in-law, who was married at the same time, bring a dowry to your brother?"

"My brother feels the same way about . . ."

"No, Monsieur Donge! I apologize for being obliged, for professional reasons, to pry into your affairs, but feelings cannot be considered in such matters. . . . The d'Onneville young ladies could not, either of them, bring you or your brother dowries, for the reason that their mother is not only almost penniless, but also entirely without property. If it had not been for certain political events, Madame d'Onneville would have enjoyed a more than respectable income. Unhappily for her, there have been many changes in Turkey since her return to France, and the securities left to her by her husband are almost worthless today. So worthless, indeed, that one of the first things she did was to mortgage her parents' house at Maufrand."

François suddenly thought of the fly struggling on the surface of the black water, but this time he was thinking not of Bébé but himself. Perspiring, he wanted to ask to have the window open, to breathe real air, to see ordinary men going by in the street, to hear other voices besides the smug voice of this lawyer.

"In short, for ten years, you and your brother have been supporting Madame d'Onneville."

Why couldn't he yell:

"To hell with you and all your gossip! All this has nothing to do with Bébé, nothing to do with us, with Chestnut Grove, with . . ."

His hands were trembling. His throat was dry. And to see the lawyer's thumb pushing snuff up his nostrils, which had dark hairs sticking out, made him feel sick.

"You understand that any case, the most insignificant as well as the most important, the case of a boundary wall as well as a crime, must be studied in all its aspects."

"My wife didn't need money."

"You gave her as much as she wanted; is that right? . . . But are you certain that the fact of your presence, the fact that you were alive, did not prevent her from spending it in the way she would have liked? Are you certain that the life she was leading with you was the life she wished to lead?"

He was almost smiling, the bearded idiot. People didn't matter to him; he saw only acts and the consequences of those acts.

"Madame d'Onneville has always liked society. She brought up her daughters in the same spirit. It is known that she constantly complains of the musty atmosphere, as she puts it, of our city. Your wife's clothes were—I won't say a scandal—but they excited comment, as did her indifference to our little society. . . . You are a businessman, Monsieur Donge . . ."

"I can swear that . . ."

"Tsk, tsk, tsk, tsk . . ."

François was surprised to hear such sounds coming out of that mouth.

"You must learn, in such matters, never to swear. . . . So then, I have established . . ."

François felt like shouting:

"You've established nothing!"

"I have established that crime for gain has not been eliminated a priori. We have examined the figures. Let us now return to the facts, and stick to the facts. . . . That particular Sunday, nothing abnormal happened, nothing exceptional. Your wife received no anonymous letters. The night before, there had been no quarrel between you."

"How do you know that?" he found the courage to ask.

The lawyer's hand, sprawling over the dossier, seemed to be caressing it.

"It is in here. We have the formal statements of my client. . . . In the same way, we know that that morning she did not even see you until lunchtime. From which I draw the conclusion that she had no more reason to poison you on that particular Sunday than on any other day.

"I will go even further . . ."

François could no longer contain himself and sprang to his feet, but with a peremptory gesture Maître Boniface made him sit down again.

"Later I will hear your objections . . . I will go even further: that Sunday there were at least three witnesses. And among those witnesses was the one your wife had reason to fear the most: your brother, whose attachment to you is well known.

"Your wife knows that you are a chemist, Monsieur Donge. Your brother, without having diplomas like you, is familiar with poisons, since you handle them daily in your business.

"Now, it is impossible to administer arsenic in one deadly dose without provoking symptoms that any-one, not just a chemist, could recognize."

He did not smile, but, pulling at his beard, looked at François with an air of satisfaction.

"Why does your wife, who is intelligent, administer such a dose on that and only on that particular day? I will tell you. Or, if you prefer, let's say that I am the public prosecutor. . . . That particular Sunday, your wife committed an error. Until then, she was always careful to put only small doses in your coffee, just enough to undermine your health little by little, pre-pare the ground. But, dazzled by the sunlight in the garden, with people so close to her, her hand was less steady. . . ."

"I swear to you that all this is . . ."

"I beg of you, Monsieur Donge! We are examining the facts, only the facts. And it is not my fault if the logical hypothesis to be drawn from them . . . I am not the one who will weigh them. That will be done by, for the most part, simple men, men who will know nothing of you or my client except what they hear in court."

At that point François, like the fly on the icy water, became motionless. He felt that he didn't have the strength to struggle. Was he still listening? Boniface's words came to him from far away, but with a distinct-ness that had something raw and implacable about it.

"The investigation is closed, as of yesterday. This morning the dossier will be turned over to the public prosecutor's office. This dossier, alas, has been established without my approval; your wife alone is responsible, because she refused to be governed by my advice.

"We might possibly have been able to plead a crime of passion without involving any third parties. . . . Your conduct, certain affairs brought up with sufficient discretion . . ."

These words were said hurriedly. Boniface, it was evident, condemned any threat to morality. His hunchbacked daughter . . . His impossible clerk . . . His dirty fingernails, and his office, as depressing as a country pharmacy, with dilapidated law books taking the place of glass jars on the equally dark and dusty shelves.

"For Monsieur Giffre, the examining magistrate, this is the first important case since he came here, and he has conducted his investigation with a prudence and sagacity to which I am pleased to pay tribute. . . . If you will permit me, I will now read you a few of my client's answers."

Was Bébé really going to appear at last, even if deformed by this terrible lawyer and by the bicycle-riding magistrate? The salmon-colored folder was half opened. Typewritten sheets appeared.

"Question: *You stated yesterday that you were not jealous of your husband and that a few months after your marriage you had given him complete freedom as far as women were concerned?*

"Answer: *On condition that he hide nothing from me . . .*"

For a second François closed his eyes. He seemed to see Bébé as she answered that question in a distinct

142

voice, sharp-featured, sitting up very straight. Boniface threw him a brief glance and continued reading.

"Question: *And has this agreement always been observed since then, on both sides?*

"Answer: *Always.*

"Question: *Did you love your husband?*

"Answer: *I don't know.*

"Question: *To put it differently, did you live as husband and wife or, as your previous statements would seem to indicate, like two friends?*

"Answer: *As husband and wife.*"

Another glance, full of curiosity this time, directed at François, who remained motionless. Naturally, Boniface would not be able to understand how one could live as . . .

"Question: *Don't these two attitudes seem to you contradictory?*

"Answer: *I didn't think so.*

"Question: *And now?*

"Answer: *I don't know.*

"Question: *You still maintain that it was not in a sudden fit of jealousy that you tried to take your husband's life?*

"Answer: *Yes.*"

"That's obvious!" François interrupted.

This time, Boniface stared at him with almost laughable amazement. But when François's face remained blank, he hastily shoved some snuff up his nose and continued:

"Question: *I am going to ask you a more precise question: If jealousy was not the motive for your crime, am I to conclude that it was hate or love?*

"Answer: *It was hate.*

"Question: *But you have already stated that you loved*

*your husband. . . . Just when did hate take the place of love?*

"Answer: *I can't tell you exactly.*

"Question: *Several years?*

"Answer: *I don't think so.*

"Question: *A year?*"

It reminded François of the confessional in his boyhood, when the priest insisted upon knowing if he had sinned through intention, thoughts, actions, or eyes.

"Answer: *I don't know.*

"Question: *Six months?*

"Answer: *Probably longer.*

"Question: *But the idea of killing him did not occur to you until you took the poison from the laboratory?*

"Answer: *I had no intention of killing him then.*

"Question: *Then what was your object?*

"Answer: *I don't know. . . . It couldn't go on. It had to be one of us, either he or I. . . . I didn't have the courage to kill myself, perhaps because of Jacques. A child needs a mother more than a father.*

"Question: *Then you had considered the question of which one of you it would be better to kill?*

"Answer: *Yes.*

"Question: *Did this debate with yourself go on for long?*

"Answer: *Several months.*

"Question: *Where did you keep the arsenic during that time?*

"Answer: *In my dressing table, at the bottom of a box of powder.*

"Question: *And each time your husband came to Chestnut Grove, you would look at him, eat with him, sleep in the same room with him, knowing that one day or other you were going to kill him?*

"Answer: *I hadn't altogether made up my mind, but I was thinking about it.*

"Question: *Could you particularize your grievances?*

"Answer: *No.*

"Question: *Did he refuse to let you have what you needed? Was he strict with you? Did he scold you? Did he beat you? Was he jealous, suspicious?*

"Answer: *He never bothered his head about me.*

"Question: *Did any third person encourage your attitude?*

"Answer: *No one.*

"Question: *What was the relationship between your mother and your husband?*

"Answer: *That of son-in-law and mother-in-law, I suppose. François put up with her without impatience and gave her money.*

"Question: *Without argument?*

"Answer: *Without too much argument.*

"Question: *Would you have given your mother more if the money had been yours?*

"Answer: *Perhaps.*

"Question: *You admit then that you made an attempt on your husband's life because you hated him, but you are unable to explain the reasons for your hate?*

"Answer: *I was suffering too much.*

"Question: *U.S. law admits a motive for divorce that our laws do not recognize; it is called mental cruelty. Do you accuse your husband of mental cruelty?*

"Answer: . . .

"Question: *That Sunday, August 20, you coldly made preparations for your husband's death. You had the paper containing arsenic with you when you went downstairs. Did you know the effects of arsenic poisoning?*

145

"Answer: *I knew it killed.*

"Question: *And you didn't think of the consequences of such an act for you?*

"Answer: *No! I had to put an end to it.*

"Question: *An end to what?*

"Answer: *I don't know. . . . It would take too long to explain . . .*

"Question: *Try.*

"Answer: *You wouldn't understand.*

"Question: *Did you have the paper of arsenic in your hand when you were putting sugar in the coffee?*

"Answer: *I had it all the time I was on the terrace. I had put it in my handkerchief.*

"Question: *You didn't feel any hesitation, any qualms?*

"Answer: *No.*

"Question: *When did you finally decide to do it?*

"Answer: *That morning, when I got up. My husband was rolling the tennis court. He was still in pajamas and slippers.*

"Question: *And the sight of him like that was enough to make you decide on his death?*

"Answer: *Yes.*

"Question: *Didn't you feel any remorse when you saw him drinking the poisoned coffee?*

"Answer: *No. I wondered if he noticed anything.*

"Question: *And did he notice anything?*

"Answer: *I suppose he thought the coffee wasn't very good. François isn't that discriminating.*"

The lawyer looked up. He wondered why his visitor seemed suddenly so agitated. It was that unexpected "François."

"Continue," François said, his nerves tense.

"You will observe that the interrogation was con-

146

ducted in a masterly fashion. This is not the first case
to pass through my hands, and I can assure you . . .
Well . . . Where were we?"

". . . *isn't that discriminating . . ."*

"Question: *After that, you awaited the outcome of your
act?*

"Answer: *Yes.*

"Question: *What did you think about?*

"Answer: *I didn't think. I said to myself that at last it
was over.*

"Question: *In short, you had a feeling of liberation?*

"Answer: *Yes.*

"Question: *From what did you feel yourself liberated?*

"Answer: *I don't know.*

"Question: *Didn't you feel yourself liberated from an
irksome servitude? That you would at last be able to live
your life according to your own ideas?*

"Answer: *That isn't it at all.*

"Question: *And when you saw him get up, seized by
the first pains, and go unsteadily toward the house?*

"Answer: *I hoped it would be over quickly.*

"Question: *You weren't afraid that your crime would
be discovered?*

"Answer: *I didn't think about it.*

"Question: *If he had died, what would you have done?*

"Answer: *Nothing. I would have gone on living with
my son.*

"Question: *At Chestnut Grove?*

"Answer: *No. I don't think so. . . . I don't know. . . .
I hadn't thought about such details. It had to be one of us
—he or I. I couldn't stand it any longer."*

Boniface was much surprised, on raising his eyes
from the dossier he had just closed, to see François

looking at him with an air of triumph. And François was suddenly chilled by the severity of the lawyer's glance.

"Well!" cried François. "You see!"

"What do I see?"

"Why . . . it seems to me . . ."

"To me, monsieur, it seems that we are faced here with a case of cynicism such as I have never met with in the whole course of my long career. I had hoped, for a while, to be able to fall back upon a plea of insanity. Unfortunately, the three specialists appointed to examine your wife, and whose opinion I respect, are categorical: Your wife is clearly responsible for her acts. At the very most, I might plead a certain morbid exaltation due to the solitude in which she lived for the last few years. . . .

"Or, if she had chosen a revolver . . ."

"But you don't understand. It's simply . . ."

Faced with such total incomprehension, François could have wept with anger. It wasn't Maître Boniface's office any longer, but a stuffy corridor in which he struggled in vain, encountering only bare walls, whose smooth surfaces offered no hold.

While they were about it, hadn't they felt, any of them—the examining magistrate with six or seven children, Maître Boniface, the public prosecutor, God knows who else—hadn't any of them felt in Bébé's answers, all so clear, so frank, so stark . . .

Though he felt it plainly, he was, alas, incapable of putting into words that thing which was pulsating, that pulse which was beating . . . that life which was longing at any price to . . .

And which found nothing around it but the cold

148

void of dark waters into which it was going to sink . . .

The consciousness that the only human being, the man who . . . During all those years, he might have . . . During all those years, a hundred, a thousand times he had had the opportunity to understand. . . . A gesture would have been enough, and . . .

She would watch his unconscious responses. He would arrive, overflowing with vitality. He would change his clothes, stretch his arms. . . . Would he, this time, at last . . .

No! Happy to have a few hours' respite, he would go out and roll the tennis court in pajamas and slippers. Or mend the kitchen faucet. Or rush to town for mushrooms. . . . Fill his time with solitary pleasure, never bothering to . . .

And when at last a little leaf had fallen, to which to cling . . . It was Mimi Lambert who brought an illusion of a personal life into the house. And he had thrown her out! . . . Why? He didn't know. Because it was *his* house . . . because he was the master . . . because he was the mate . . .

He alone, even if he wasn't there.

"So you wanted to be married, did you? So much the worse for you, young lady. Just remember you've married a Donge, and the Donges . . ."

Jeanne had escaped because Jeanne hadn't loved enough. Committees, milk foundations, layette societies were enough to absorb her vital energy and restore equilibrium.

The whole trouble came from the fact that Bébé, unlike Jeanne, had loved. Loved to the point of complete, irremediable despair. And he had never noticed.

149

"Since you have forgiven your wife, Monsieur Donge, and desire her acquittal, as an attorney, all I can say . . ."

As a man, Boniface judged them, both of them, more severely than any judge could possibly judge them. Once more he began pushing snuff up his nose.

"It is difficult for me to tell you at this time what my defense will be. It will depend on the composition of the jury, as well as on the nature of the public prosecutor's case. . . . However, I must in all frankness admit that I am confronted by an extremely difficult task and that . . ."

François never remembered how he finally got out of that trap. Boniface must have opened the door for him. The moment he looked at the daylight outside and took a breath of different air, he rushed away. Without even muttering the usual polite formulas.

In the street there was sunlight, dust in the sunlight, a vegetable vendor with a dog harnessed to his little cart.

In the United States, the examining magistrate had said . . .

What was the expression he used?

*Mental cruelty.*

François stepped on the starter several times, having forgotten to turn on the ignition.

Bébé had said:

"It had to be one of us, either he or I. . . . A child needs a mother more than a father. . . ."

He had forgotten that it was market day. He kept blowing his horn at the corner of a crowded street.

"Can't you read?" one of the countrywomen

shouted at him, pointing to a sign that was always stuck between two paving stones on market days. "You're not allowed through here."

He had to back up and make innumerable maneuvers to turn around.

# − *9* −

He recognized the landscape. He had been on this road before, with Félix. They had left Millau at dusk. They had stopped there to buy gloves, because Millau was famous for gloves. The foreman of the cheese-making plant was also named Millau.

To reach Cahors, François crossed a vast stony plateau without a house, without a tree, a desert of pebbles such as might be expected on the moon.

Why was he in such a hurry today? It wasn't his fault if he had forgotten why. He did his best to remember. Did his best! Who had said that? Apparently his best wasn't enough. True, he was still weak. No, really, he couldn't say why he was in a hurry.

It must be dusk now too, because the light was the same as that other time, or, rather, there was an absence of light, which was, nevertheless, not darkness.

The light came from nowhere. The pebbles were the same gray as the sky.

Between night and day, he was both hot and cold. Perspiring and shivering. He kept the accelerator pressed down to the floorboards, yet the car seemed to advance at a snail's pace.

Was he going to pass without seeing *her*, or pretend not to see *her*? He knew that Bébé was there on the left in the little white car. She was wearing a green chiffon dress with a skirt to the ankles, a picture hat of pale straw, and she carried a parasol. The idea of encumbering oneself with a parasol in a car! And it was an open car. It looked like Mimi Lambert's.

"Well, it's her concern."

She was frantically waving to him with her parasol. But why had she taken the white car? Why had she risked going all alone into this desert of the moon? Why had she started along that little road to the left of the highway, since there was no possible way of ever getting off it again?

Bébé's car had broken down. Well, what of it? He was in a hurry. . . . God! How could he have forgotten where he was going and what it was he had to do?

Was he going to pass the little road, pretending not to see his wife? It wouldn't be very gallant, nor even polite. Old man Donge may have been a tanner, but, all the same, he had taught his sons manners.

"Hello! Hello, Bébé!"

That's the way! Casually, without stopping, without slowing down, as though he didn't know her car had broken down. She kept waving her parasol. Too late! He had passed her. He couldn't be expected to see behind him. . . .

153

How long would she stay there? He hadn't a minute to lose. He had a pressing appointment. The proof: a great crowd waiting for him.

There were more than a hundred people in the hall, some of whom he knew, others he didn't know. There were workmen from his factory, the waiter at the Café du Centre, the one who at New Year's gave him a little bottle of liqueur and an advertisement pencil. . . .

"Sit down."

"First, I must explain, Monsieur le Roy . . ."

"Tsk, tsk, tsk . . . I tell you to sit down."

Had everyone else recognized Maître Boniface too? It changed him, being dressed like a king, but that was certainly his beard, only smoother, and his bushy eyebrows. He wore a king's costume—a red robe, a crown on his head—and held a scepter. When he said: "Tsk, tsk, tsk," he gave François little blows on his shoulder with his scepter, and his face, the florid red of a king on a playing card, expressed hilarity.

That, of course, was why the others didn't recognize him: because of his ruddy complexion and his Rabelaisian smile.

"Eh, my boy . . ."

"I'm not your . . ."

"Tsk, tsk, tsk."

And bang! A whack of the scepter on his head. Then, looking down, François saw with horror that he had nothing on but undershorts. They should have given him time to dress. He couldn't appear before the king in undershorts. He lost all his self-possession.

"Monsieur le Roy . . ."

"Silence! And silence over there too, at the back . . ."

François turned and could see nothing but heads, hundreds of heads; more people must have come in to fill the enormous room, which had the same dark woodwork as Boniface's office.

". . . mental cruelty. You have been found guilty of mental cruelty, my boy. Ha! Ha! The court sentences you to twenty years in the hospital. Sister Adonie, remove the prisoner!"

"Monsieur! Monsieur! . . . It's eight o'clock!"

Angèle, the old servant at Quai des Tanneurs, was bustling about the room.

"What suit shall I get out? . . . You'd better take a bath. . . . What a messy bed! You must have thrashed around all night."

"What's the weather?"

"It's raining."

A black suit? A bit exaggerated, perhaps. He would like . . . A gray suit?

Besides, it wasn't certain that he'd appear in court. Boniface had begged him to stay home.

"You haven't been called as a witness, by either the prosecution or the defense. I would much prefer to use your previous declarations, as the need arises, than to have you in court. . . . If the judge avails himself of his discretionary powers and decides to hear you, I can always telephone. Stay home."

It was almost like the day of a funeral. The house seemed to be full of unusual drafts. The old servant had been crying. She talked to him as to a man in deep mourning.

"You must eat something. It will give you strength."

He had given his employees the day off. He felt the emptiness of the offices and missed the familiar noises of the tannery.

Then Félix arrived in his car, with Jeanne—a serious, worried Félix, who, after an anxious glance at François, kissed him on both cheeks.

"How *are* you?"

Félix had dressed more carefully than usual. Jeanne too, and she had decided to wear black. Both had been called as witnesses and were on their way to the courthouse.

"You'll stay calm, François, won't you?" Jeanne insisted. "I am sure everything will turn out for the best. . . . By the way, I had a telegram from Mother."

She handed him the slip of blue paper.

*"Violent attack of rheumatism stop Impossible travel stop Sent Boniface medical certificate and written deposition stop Telegraph outcome stop Love Mother."*

They glanced at the clock. Ten minutes to nine. The trial was to begin at nine.

"As soon as you've been heard, you'll telephone, won't you, Félix?"

Marthe arrived, having come by bus from Chestnut Grove. She too had been called as a witness. Jacques was to remain in the country with Clo.

"We'll see you later."

They tried to smile, without success. A fine rain was sprinkling the windows. Only a few yellow leaves still clung to the black branches of the trees along the quay. Directly in front of the house, a fisherman,

156

dangling a line in the water, sat very still, hunched up in oilskins, his eyes glued to his cork surrounded by expanding circles.

"Monsieur should do something, anything, so the time won't seem so long."

Having slept too little and dreamed too much, his head was empty, his face feverish. He kept passing back and forth in front of the telephone, hoping for a call, hoping they would tell him to hurry over to the courthouse.

"Two sessions will be enough," Maître Boniface had declared. "Inasmuch as my client has made a full confession, the state has decided not to hear some of its witnesses. I would have done the same. The fewer witnesses there are, the easier it will be for the defense. It leaves us a free field."

François had suggested that he wait in a little café near the courthouse.

"You are too well known in town. It would get around. People would consider it undignified."

What was it Boniface had made him write at his dictation? François had resisted. He found the formulas ridiculous, and so far from the reality!

*"With all my heart and soul, before God and before man . . ."*

"But, don't you think . . . ?"

"Write what I tell you. It's the style that appeals to juries."

*"I forgive my wife the harm she has done me and the harm that she tried to do me."*

"Listen, Maître Boniface. I have nothing to forgive, since I feel that . . ."

"Do you or don't you wish to aid the defense?"

*"I realize that the solitude and ennui in which I left a young woman accustomed to a more brilliant life . . ."*

"You don't think that if I appeared as witness, and if . . ."

"You would talk to them the way you have talked to me, and no one would understand. Attempting to whitewash your wife, you'd only risk doing the contrary. . . . Give me your letter."

He trembled, and rushed to the ringing telephone.

"Hello! François Donge, yes . . . Impossible! The office is closed today. You ought to know that. . . . No, I can't possibly take an order. . . ."

Still holding the receiver, he glanced at the clock. Nine-forty-five! The reading of the indictment must be over by now. François knew that it was not more than ten typewritten pages.

Special passes had had to be distributed. All the city's society women were there, and Bébé, pale and dignified, as though in church. Boniface must have told her that François would not be in the courtroom, that he had forbidden him to come, but wouldn't she automatically look for him in the crowd anyway?

The jurors, on one side, sat in neat rows, as if posing for a picture, and in their Sunday best, like the photograph of the master tanners. . . .

"Monsieur really should find something to do—anything at all."

Half past ten and no telephone call yet! He went down to his office, then upstairs again, went down again, and opened the door to the street.

"Monsieur knows very well that . . ." panted the old woman, who had hurried after him.

She thought he was going to leave, and she had been told to keep an eye on him. But he only wanted to get a breath of fresh air. It was October, and chilly. The fisherman was still there. Children went by in hooded rain capes that made them look like gnomes.

"Isn't that the telephone?"

"It's the alarm clock in my room."

Finally, at quarter after eleven, a car stopped at the curb, Félix's car.

"Well?"

"Nothing. Everything went smoothly. . . . Seems the jury isn't bad, except for the pharmacist. Maître Boniface had already challenged five, so he didn't dare challenge him too. . . . Naturally, it's the pharmacist they've named foreman of the jury."

Félix seemed to have come from another world.

"And Bébé?"

"Perfect. She hasn't changed. . . . She's put on a little weight, if anything. . . . When she came in, everyone seemed to stop breathing."

"How is she dressed?"

"She had on her navy-blue suit and a small dark hat. She looked as if she were entering a salon for a formal reception. She seated herself with perfect composure. Then she looked around the room as if . . ."

Félix's throat tightened.

"And the public prosecutor?"

"A big man, with boils. . . . He was tough, but less so than might have been expected. . . . In short, so far everything has been very simple. Even routine:

" 'No further questions to ask the witness?'

" 'No questions.'

" 'And you, Maître?'

159

" 'No questions.'

"In fact, the witnesses were plainly disappointed to have been summoned for so little. They hesitated to leave the witness stand. . . . One woman seemed so determined to stay in the chair that the spectators burst out laughing and the judge had to insist:

" 'Madame, you have been told to leave!'

"She finally departed, muttering a whole string of complaints."

It wasn't long before Jeanne too returned, in a taxi.

"How do you feel, François? . . . I wonder if, all things considered, it wouldn't have been better for you to come too. It's much simpler than one imagines. . . . I was afraid it would be awfully upsetting. But it isn't a bit. When I took the witness stand, Bébé made me a little sign with her hand that nobody else would notice . . . like this, just raising two fingers. . . . The way we used to when we were children, at the table, and wanted to send some secret message to each other . . . I could almost swear she was smiling. . . . Come, children, let's eat! Félix has to be at the courthouse again at one-thirty, when the court reconvenes."

A noise of knives and forks in the silence, again like a meal on the day of a funeral.

"Do they still expect to finish today?"

"That depends on the public prosecutor. Maître Boniface insists that his own summation won't take more than an hour. But apparently he always makes the same promise, which doesn't prevent him from talking for two or three hours if he feels he has a receptive audience."

Félix left. Jeanne stayed behind.

160

"Tell me, François . . . It isn't too soon to consider certain details. . . . I knock on wood. . . . If she's acquitted, she'll want to see Jacques right away. Don't you think it would be unwise to take her out to Chestnut Grove? I'm afraid it might bring back memories. Do you know what I suggest? . . . We'll take the car. I'll drive, because I'm afraid you're too nervous. We'll go and get Jacques and take everything he'll need for the night. . . . If you like, we'll bring Clo too. . . . In an hour, we can be back. Boniface certainly won't need you before then."

It wasn't yet three o'clock. He finally agreed. They drove through the rain. The road was deserted. The windshield wiper was working badly, and Jeanne had to lean forward to see ahead.

"As soon as Félix telephones, you should go to the courthouse and leave your car in front of the little door on Rue des Moines."

The white gate. Clo came running, thinking it was news, perhaps even madame herself!

"Get the boy ready, Clo. Pack everything he'll need for the night."

"Where's Mama?"

"You'll surely see her tonight. . . ."

"She won't be convicted?"

While Jacques was being dressed, François wandered through the house, which no longer seemed to belong to him. He felt that he was definitely moving out, that he was abandoning it forever.

"Suppose I telephone."

"Where?"

"To the house . . ."

He gave the number.

161

"Is that you, Angèle? . . . This is Monsieur Donge. Has anyone telephoned? . . . You're sure? You haven't been away? . . . Good! We'll be back in half an hour. Is the boy's room ready? . . . Light some logs, yes; it's quite raw."

The day went by more quickly than might have been expected. Maître Boniface was probably in the middle of his summation, his nose full of snuff, his sleeves unfurled, his raised voice echoing in the farthest corners of the court. Young lawyers, older attorneys would be standing and listening near the witnesses' entrance.

"You ought to have a whiskey, François."

Jacques was in the kitchen chattering with old Angèle.

"Do you know what she's done, my mama? They won't dare convict her, will they? Because that would be a miscarriage of justice. Marthe said so. . . ."

Marthe came back soaking wet. She had left her umbrella in the witnesses' room.

"Maître Boniface is talking now," she announced, blowing her nose. "Lots of people are crying. . . . Monsieur Félix sent me home to tell you everything was going well. . . ."

"No, François. Don't go yet!"

But he couldn't stand it any longer. He put on his coat and looked around feverishly for his hat. It was dark outside. He forgot to turn on his lights, and was stopped by a policeman at the bridge.

When he arrived at the courthouse square, people were milling around in front, gathering in little groups

162

to talk; it was like an intermission at the theater. He gathered that the jury had retired to deliberate. Parked by the curb, he remained sitting behind the wheel, afraid of being recognized. He saw Félix, bareheaded and without a coat, coming out of the tobacco shop. Félix recognized the car.

"I've just phoned. We'll know in a few minutes. . . . You shouldn't have come."

"What's the general opinion?"

"Not bad . . . Boniface made a magnificent plea. . . . It seems that it's a good sign if the jury is out a long time. But if they come back in a few minutes . . . Stay in the car, François. . . . Do you want me to get you a drink?"

"No. And Bébé?"

"Always the same . . . Did Marthe tell you that women were crying in the courtroom? Boniface described at length her life at Constantinople, her family, her . . ."

François's fingers suddenly gripped Félix's arm. People were hurrying back into the courthouse. The next moment they learned it was a false alarm. The jury was still out.

Félix, to distract his brother, kept on talking, scarcely knowing what he was saying, reeling off sentences at random.

"He dwelt at length on the unpreparedness of the youth of today to meet reality, and the consequences of an education that neglects . . ."

The wet square showed bright splashes of reflected light. Reporters were telephoning their papers from the corner café. A well-dressed middle-aged man came and peered through the car window, and only went

163

away when he saw the two brothers looking at him.

The next moment, he was talking to a group of people on the courthouse steps and pointing at the car.

"Promise me you'll stay here, François. It wouldn't do if, when the verdict . . ."

This time a bell rang, once more a reminder of the theater. People began to push their way into the courthouse. Dark silhouettes hurried through the puddles.

"You won't budge now, will you?"

A car drew up behind them. It was Jeanne, too impatient to wait at home for the news.

"Is this the verdict?"

François nodded.

"Pull up a few yards. There'll be a mob here shortly. I'll show you a side entrance."

A gothic door, like that of a sacristy. Without a guard. A few worn steps, then an unlighted corridor, more like an underground passage. The behind-the-scenes of the law courts.

"François, where are you going?"

He had gone through the door in spite of himself. Alarmed, Jeanne followed him. The corridor made a sharp turn. Suddenly they ran into the human element again, animal warmth. People were tightly packed against a door guarded by a gendarme. From underneath the door came a streak of light.

Beyond that door was a crowd in hushed suspense. A voice, trying to sound assured, suddenly rose distinctly, separating each syllable:

"First question: yes."

The first question was:

"Did the defendant act with intent to kill?"

"Second question: yes."

That was the question of premeditation. François had had some difficulty understanding Maître Boniface's explanation on this subject. The lawyer had said:

"Even if the jury answers yes to the first question, they may possibly answer no to the second."

"But my wife admits premeditation."

"That makes no difference. It is a question of determining the severity of the sentence. In answering no to this second question, the jurors lighten the sentence by one degree."

A clamor of voices in the courtroom. Jeanne's hand in the darkness found François's and squeezed it.

A bell . . . Call to order . . .

"Third question: yes."

The crowd around them stirred with excitement. So, the jury had conceded extenuating circumstances!

"François, stay here!"

But even if François had wanted to rush into the courtroom, the gendarme would have prevented him.

A silence. The noise of shuffling feet. During the few moments the judges would take to deliberate, the crowd would be moving toward the entrance. If the trial had lasted two hours longer, if it had lasted all night, no one would have left. But now that they knew the verdict . . .

"Be calm, François."

Jeanne was quietly weeping. They could not see each other. They still could see only that streak of light under the door and the faint glint of silver braid on the gendarme's uniform.

"The court having deliberated . . ."

165

The shuffling suddenly stopped. Everyone stood still.

". . . sentences . . ."

A sob. It was Jeanne, although she had sworn not to break down. She still gripped François's moist hand.

". . . to five years at hard labor . . ."

A strange noise, something like that of a wave rasping back over a pebbly beach. The crowd reacting to the verdict. Some people left. Others lingered in the courtroom, where half the lights were quickly turned off.

"Come!"

Jeanne knew her way around the building by this time. She hurried down a corridor and opened a door into a little room with nothing in it but a long bench, and bare stone walls. Another door, opposite them, was open. They could see the judges leaving the courtroom in single file. Bébé appeared, came down three steps, followed by two gendarmes and by Maître Boniface, waving his black wings.

Then everything disappeared: the open door, the bit of empty courtroom, the representatives of the law, and the attorney in his robes. Only Jeanne was still there.

Soon nobody seemed to be there but Bébé, standing in the dim light, the mysterious half-veil of her blue hat covering the upper part of her face.

"You were there?" she asked.

And then immediately:

"Where is Jacques?"

"He's at the house. I thought . . ."

He couldn't speak. His throat was too tight, and each word felt big and rough as a peach stone.

He held his hands out toward his wife's white hands.

"Forgive me, Bébé . . . I . . ."

"You're here too, Jeanne?"

The two sisters fell into each other's arms, or, rather, it was Jeanne who, sobbing, fell into Bébé's arms.

"You mustn't cry. Will you tell Marthe? . . . But she'll surely come to see me tomorrow. . . . I have inquired; I'll be here at least a week before they take me to Haguenau."

François was listening. A scene came back to him from a film he had seen with . . . Why did it have to be with Olga? Women in gray uniforms and sabots were walking in single file and silently taking their places, like phantoms, at long work tables. Their hair was cut short. The moment one of them raised her head, a prison matron . . .

What did it matter if Maître Boniface was there and the two gendarmes? Personal pride no longer counted.

"Forgive me . . . I have finally understood. . . . I was hoping . . ."

He looked at her eyes, shaded by the thin veil. They were calm, serious. Now she was shaking her head. She was no longer a woman like other women. She seemed to him as inaccessible as the Virgin must have seemed to the early Christians.

"It wouldn't have helped any, François. You see, it's too late. It's broken. . . . I didn't realize myself how completely. . . . When you drank your coffee, I watched you. I watched you with curiosity, only curiosity. Already, for me, you no longer existed. . . . And when you got up with your hand pressed to your side and hurried toward the house, my only thought was, I hope it's over quickly."

"Broken . . ."

"Perhaps I shouldn't have told you that, but it's better. I explained it all to Maître Boniface. . . .

"I waited too long, hoped too long. . . .

"The only thing I ask of you is that you keep Marthe for Jacques. She's used to him. She knows what to do. . . . Maître Boniface, I want to thank you. You did all that was possible. I know that if I had listened to your advice from the beginning . . . But I didn't want to be acquitted. . . . What was that?"

She gave a start. A flashbulb had gone off. A photographer had succeeded in sneaking into the room.

"Good-by, Jeanne. Good-by, François."

She was ready to walk away between her guards to the prison van waiting for her in the courtyard.

"You should apply for a divorce and begin your life over again. . . . There's no reason why, just because we failed, the two of us . . . You have such vitality!"

Those were the last words he heard her speak.

". . . such vitality!"

She said it with envy, with regret.

A door . . . Footsteps . . .

"Come."

But it was Jeanne who hesitated and threw herself on François's chest.

"It isn't possible! No! Bébé . . . Our Bébé! . . . François! Don't let her go."

François mechanically patted his sister-in-law's shoulder, while Maître Boniface, giving a little cough, stepped aside.

"François! Bébé at Haguenau! . . . Why don't you say something? Why do you let them do it? . . . François! . . . No! I can't bear it. . . ."

She didn't want to leave. It was François who had to drag her away. Outside, they found a frantic Félix waiting for them.

"My poor François!"

No! No! Not poor François! There was no poor François!

There was simply . . .

What was there? It was impossible to explain, even to Félix, even to Jeanne.

His turn now—that's what there was. . . . She had passed by up there on the lunar plateau. He was gesticulating. He was calling her. . . .

"Too late, my poor François."

She was in a hurry. She was swept headlong by the force of circumstances. . . .

There was nothing for him to do but wait in solitude for her second passage, if she ever passed again. Nothing to do but listen for sounds, for footsteps, for the shock of meteors. And the sound of cars that . . .

"You'd better go in his car with him, and drive."

It was Jeanne's voice. A sidewalk, rain, the sign over a little café where men were playing Russian pool.

As though he weren't able to drive himself! But why worry them?

"You shouldn't have brought Jacques. Now we'll have to . . ."

"I want to spend the night at Chestnut Grove," François said.

"But it's eight o'clock. . . ."

169

"What difference does it make? I'll take Jacques and Marthe. I'll drive slowly."

To win over his son! And then . . .

"He's not the same man since Bébé . . ."

People didn't know. People never understood. Was it perhaps because if people understood, life wouldn't be possible?

"You better see Monsieur Félix. . . . Nowadays, he's the one who . . ."

Maître Boniface, his shirt filthy and his nose full of snuff, had declared:

"Five years? . . . One moment! Three months already served awaiting trial represents six months of the actual sentence. And then, with good behavior and a presidential pardon . . . say three years, even less . . ."

François was counting the days. It couldn't be helped if the Bébé who came back . . .

At least she would be here.

She would be here!

And even if, as she had been honest enough to tell him, she . . .

"It would be better if you saw his brother, Félix. . . ."